The Adolescent And The Cartel

The Adolescent And The Cartel

Intrigue in the Adirondack

A work of fiction by H. G. Nowland

iUniverse, Inc.
New York Bloomington Shanghai

The Adolescent And The Cartel
Intrigue in the Adirondack

iUniverse books may be ordered through booksellers or by contacting:

iUniverse
1663 Liberty Drive
Bloomington, IN 47403
www.iuniverse.com
1-800-Authors (1-800-288-4677)

ISBN: 978-0-595-48593-2 (pbk)
ISBN: 978-0-595-71981-5 (cloth)
ISBN: 978-0-595-60686-3 (ebk)

Printed in the United States of America

Acknowledgements

I would like to express my sincere appreciation to Dr. Donald Morrison and to my brother Melvin (Mel) Nowland for their invaluable assistance on this book. Their assistance has helped me avoid many technical errors and I am sure has increased the realism of this story.

Preface

John Davidson is a Vietnam veteran who has experienced nightmares of his war experiences since his return from Vietnam. He also has never forgiven himself for a number of his actions while in Vietnam. His problems destroyed his marriage and drove him to alcoholism and, finally, he became a street person. After an experience on the street caused him to seek help in recovering, he moved, deep in the woods, to a cabin he built himself. He writes to support himself. Mostly he writes westerns and sometimes mysteries. He avoids contact with people as much as possible. Most of his supplies are available in the small town a couple dozen miles to the South. Most of the research he needs to do is also available at the library there. His life of isolation and solitude is rudely altered when a preteen girl suddenly enters his life. The girl has problems of her own. Problems that make John's own problems pale in comparison to hers'. John soon finds himself caught up in these problems. He will need to use all his street smarts, woodsman knowledge, military training and even some of the things he learned as a boy scout if he is to save his own life and the life of his little friend.

Chapter 1

From Humdrum to Bedlam

Maybe my eyes are deceiving me, but this is the second time in the last thirty minutes or so that I have seen something red dart from one tree to another. I have been working at my computer for over three hours now without a break. Maybe I need to take a break before I start seeing Santa Claus outside in the rain.

I stand up, walk over to the door and push it open for a few minutes. The cold air refreshes me in almost no time. As I start to close the door I see that flash of red again. I thought "it was too early for Santa Claus to be in the neighborhood. After all it is not even Thanksgiving yet". This time I am amazed to see the flash is a girl and not too big a girl at that. I guess I had better get on my rain coat and go out to see if I can find her. I hate being out in the rain. I had enough of it in Nam. What is a girl doing up here anyway? It is miles to the nearest road and the nearest cabin is nearly as far.

I pull on my raincoat and slip on my old ball cap before stepping though the door. Standing on the porch I call out to the girl, who is nowhere to be seen. "Come on up here out of the rain," I yell. There is no answer. I wait another minute or so and then call out again. "Come up here where it is warm and dry before you catch your death of the cold." Still I get no answer. Oh well, I guess I'll have to get wet. I sure was hoping I could avoid doing so.

I step off the porch and start walking in the direction where I last saw her moving. After walking about a dozen yards I stop and listen. I hear a slight clicking sound. It is coming from behind me. I turn and see the small figure clad in a bright red coat, huddled nearly in a ball shape, snuggled down between two trees. It appears she has pulled leaves up over her in an effort of concealment.

"Come on out of there," I say in a rather irritated tone. "We need to get you inside and dried off. You are going to die of hyperthermia if you don't.

After a few seconds I hear a small voice say, "Just go ahead and kill me here. There is no sense in waiting."

"Kill you? What are you talking about kid? I'm just trying to help you out so quit with the dumb statements and come on out, will you? I am getting all wet too and to say the least I am not enjoying it."

"I'm not going anywhere with you of my own free will so come on over and get me if you want me," she says in a defiant tone of voice I didn't even think a girl that small could muster up.

"I'm not going to drag you anywhere Kid. I'm going back to my cabin where it's dry and warm. You are welcome to come too, if you wish. If you prefer not to come into my cabin then you can walk to the nearest cabin down the hill and to the south. It is only about a four mile walk and I am not sure the Wagner's are even there now. They only use their cabin on holidays and vacations. Going up hill like you were heading will get you nowhere. My cabin is the highest one on this slope. Now I am going inside and get warm. If you are smart you will come in with me," is my retort as I turn and start walking back toward the cabin.

"How did you find me anyway? You had already walked past me", she says with a still defiant tone in her voice.

"Your teeth," I answer.

"My what?

"Your teeth. They are chattering so loud they sound like a machine gun. Now are you going to cut out this nonsense and come inside with me," I ask as I again turn and start walking back toward the cabin. It is all starting to come back to me now why I move so far away from people. People are a pain!

As I start walking up the steps to my porch I glance back to where I had left the girl. She is now standing, but she hasn't made a move toward me or the cabin. Our constitution guarantees our rights and I guess this includes the right to be stupid so I continue on up the steps, across the porch and into my cabin.

Now I am all wet. Water has dripped down my neck and is running down my back. I pull my cap and raincoat off and throw them onto the old rocking chair. After throwing another log on the fire I turn my back to it so my shirt will dry. Suddenly, I hear a noise at the door. When I glance over I see the door slowly opening. A short, slim figure slowly enters the cabin. She is clad in a full length red cloth coat that is so soaking wet that it must weigh more than her. She is wearing jeans and tennis shoes. Not exactly the best attire for a trek in the woods.

I look over to her and say, "Take that coat off and come over in front of the fire so you can get warm and dry."

"Don't be telling me what to do," she responds with a snarl on her face meaner than a junkyard dog's.

"Okay I won't. Just do what you want," I say then I mutter, mostly to myself, "You're even worse than my daughters."

"Your daughters! You have daughters?"

"Yes, I have a couple of daughters or at least I did a long time ago," I say begrudging having said anything.

Slowly the small figure starts moving toward me and the fire. At about four or five paces from me she pulls her hand from under her coat. She is holding a butcher knife. She points it toward me and says, "You stay away from me."

"Now where did you get the knife anyway or do you always go around with a butcher knife under your coat?" I ask the question though I am not sure that I want to hear the answer.

"My Mother gave it to me when we left the car. She has one too."

"Your Mother is up here too?"

"Yes, and if you try to do anything to me she will come and use her knife on you."

"Listen Kid, I mean no harm to you and I hope you have the same intentions toward me. So I am going to move away from the fire and you can move in close to it and get warm," I say as I walk back over to my desk and shutdown my computer. If I am not going to be writing there is no sense in allowing the battery to run down.

When I glance back toward the girl she has removed her coat and is standing in front of the fire shaking like a leaf during a tornado. Every stitch of her cloths is soaked. Before I think I say, "Get out of those wet things before you catch your death."

"If you think I am going to strip in front of an old man like you, you had better just forget it" she says with that junkyard dog snarl on her face again.

"Okay then, go on over to the bathroom and undress. There are towels on the shelf. Get yourself one and dry off. You can use another one to cover yourself," I say as I point toward the bathroom.

I've seen snails that move faster than she moves toward the bathroom. She moves sideways away from the fireplace, which is in the center of the room, and then walks backward toward the bathroom still clutching her knife. I move over to the cupboard and get out a can of soup to heat. I don't know about the kid, but I am starting to get hungry.

Suddenly I hear a yell from the bathroom, "Hey, what kind of a bathroom is this anyway? There's no door."

"I built this cabin for myself and not for anyone else to live in so there was not a lot of need to provide for modesty. Now I am on the other side of the cabin and I promise that I will not look your way so go on and get dried off. I am fixing some soup. You can have some if you want," I say while continuing with making ready the soup.

I set a bowl of hot soup and a spoon on the hearth and then go back to the table with my bowl. A short time later I hear a slurping sound from near the hearth. I glance over to see the small figure wrapped in a towel eating soup, her knife lying nearby. Just in case she needs it I guess. Oh well, if it makes her more comfortable then what the heck. At least she is no longer shaking so violently.

CHAPTER 2

THE TRUTH STARTS TO EMERGE

Neither of us says anything while we eat our soup. After I am finished with my bowl I ask, "Do you have a name or do I just keep calling you Kid?"

"You can call me Ginger. What do I call you or shall I just keep calling you Old Man," she replies this time speaking in an almost civil tone of voice.

"I'm John," I reply". Then I go on to say, "I'll make up the top bunk for you to sleep in Ginger."

"If you built this place only for yourself how come you have bunk beds", she asks with a tone of logic in her voice?

"I have a buddy who comes up and stays with me sometimes. He likes to hunt so I let him stay here and hunt on my land," I say as I start pulling a couple of blankets out of my footlocker.

"Oh I can't stay here," Ginger says showing fear in her eyes and I know what fear looks like having seen it on so many faces in Nam.

"And just why can't you stay?"

"Because they will be here soon and they will kill me if they find me. They'll most likely do the same to you. They don't like to leave anyone around to talk," she adds as an after thought.

"Okay, I think you better let me in on what this is all about. If you go back out in the woods again you will die just as surly as if someone shoots you. In fact being shot would be a lot less painful way to go than to die of exposure in the woods."

"You don't have to get involved in this. This is my problem and I will handle it myself," she says again looking like a snarling dog.

"From what you've said so far, it sounds like I am already involved in whatever it is you are running from. If I am going to get killed it sure would be nice to know what I am going to die for."

"They killed my Dad and now there are trying to kill my Mom and me."

"Oh, I'm sorry about your Dad Kid"

"Hey, it isn't any big deal. He wasn't much of a dad anyway."

"Come on Kid, give him some credit. If it hadn't been for him you wouldn't be here now, you know."

"Yeah, but that's about all he ever did. He was never around much and when he was he didn't waste much of his time on me," Ginger says almost spitting the words out as if they didn't taste good.

"Who killed your dad, anyway?"

"Mom said it was the people he worked for. That's all I know about it."

I wanted to ask her more. But decided my time might be better spent trying to find out how much danger we might be in and how soon we can expect it to be upon us.

"How many people are after you?"

"I don't know."

"Make a guess if you don't know. We need to have some idea of what we are up against," I ask starting to get a little impatient with all the answers Ginger is giving me that are telling me nothing.

"It looked like there were four in the SUV that was following us," she says, more like she is asking a question than answering one.

"Us, is that you and your mom?" I ask trying to shed a little light on what she is telling me.

"Yeah, that's me and Mom. These guys have been watching our house and following us everywhere we go every since Dad was killed. Yesterday, Mom packed the car with everything she felt we would need while it was parked in the garage where these guys couldn't see it. This morning we got into the car and backed out of the drive. When we started down the street they followed just like Mom knew they would. She started toward Grandma and Granddad's place. Twice, when no other cars were in sight, they tried to force Mom off on a side road. Mom out maneuvered them both times. She knew we couldn't keep this up for too long without being forced onto a side road or having an accident trying to avoid them. Finally, she got onto the Interstate highway and turned back toward home. She exited at the first rest stop she came to. She wanted to get us to where other people were around. She said she didn't think they would do anything where they would be seen doing it. The problem was there was no one else around so we went like we were going into the women's room. As soon as we were out of their site Mom grabbed my hand and we ran into the woods behind the rest stop. This didn't fool them for long though. We could hear them following us. We came to a fork in the path we were following. Mom told me to hide in the bushes, gave me the knife and she took the path to the left. She said that I should wait until these guys passed and then I should take the path to the right. I did what she told me to do and that is how I ended up here."

"Tell me, what makes you so sure these guys want to kill you anyway?"

"Mostly because they shot at me twice on the way up here," She says with near panic in her voice. Then she goes on to say, "Get your gun out so you can shoot them when they get here."

"I'm sorry to tell you Kid, but there is no gun. After Nam I just didn't have too much use for firearms anymore."

Never short for a comeback the kid says, "What good are you to me if you don't even have a gun?

"Give me some credit Kid. I survived a couple of tours in Vietnam so I must know something about survival," I say, trying to reassure the kid a bit, but I am not too sure it reassures me very much. She is right about them, whoever "them" may be; having guns and us having none puts us at a definite disadvantage.

"Okay you stay away from the windows. I am going out on the porch and have a quick look around." After a few minutes on the porch it is plain that either there is no one outside near the cabin or they are well hidden if they are here.

As soon as I walk back inside the kid starts to mouth off again by saying, "Did you see anything or are your old eyes so weak that you wouldn't see anything if it was out there?"

"Hey Kid," but before I can say anymore she butts in again.

"Quit calling me Kid. I told you my name is Ginger."

"Well, Ginger may be your name but, somehow, Kid seems to fit you better. So you had better get used to being call Kid. Okay?" Even before I give her time to respond I say, "I'm going up in the loft. I have some observation slits up there. If anybody is around here I'll be able to see them moving and they won't have any idea they are being watched."

"What are you doing with observation slots?" the Kid lips off. Then she goes on to ask, "Are you one of those peeping toms my mother told me about?"

"No, I am not a peeping tom. There is nobody out here to peep at. I use these observation slots to observe animals. Some day I hope to write a book on the behavior of wild animals."

"Yeah man, I'm sure, as if you could even write."

By now I have had enough of the kid's lip so I just start up the stairs to the loft. I guess the kid is about out of lip too. She doesn't say anything more. I stare through first one and then another observation slot for about thirty minutes or maybe even more without seeing anything out of the ordinary. I see no need to continue watching. It is getting dark now even though it is too early in the day to be this dark. My guess is it is about to rain again or maybe as cold as it is it will come as snow.

When I come back downstairs I see why the kid isn't giving me any lip. She is sitting in a chair, at the table, with her head lying on the table. She is sound asleep.

I have a bit of a dilemma on my hands. I can't take the kid with me and go looking for her mother. I fear she can't stand to get cold and wet again. If someone is following the kid and she is truly in danger I can't very well walk off and leave her here. Besides as dark as it is getting it would be unlikely I could find her. It would be more likely that I might injure myself than to find the kid's mother. Oh well if she keeps walking in the direction the kid said she will end up at the Wagner's place. Even if they are not there she will be able to find shelter on their porch. I fear there is little we can do before morning.

This is about the time I usually start up the generator so I can charge the batteries for my computer, flashlights, etc. I usually run it three or four hours to provide me lights during the evening and to keep my refrigerator and freezer from warming up too much. It also runs the pump that pumps water into my storage tank up the hill. I don't like to run it any more than necessary. It is too much of a hassle getting gasoline up here.

I walk out to the little shed where the generator is located and crank it up. On my way back in I close the shutters over the windows. I only use the shutters when the wind is up. I sure don't need any limbs blowing down and break the glass in one of my windows.

I walk over and pick Ginger up and carry her over to the lower bunk. I am shocked at how little she weighs. I guess I thought spunk weighed more. She sure is full of spunk anyway. She flinches a little when I put a blanket over her, but she never wakes up.

I start punching the keys on my computer again. I am a little behind on meeting the deadline my publisher set for me. I don't know why I let him set deadlines for my work. After all, that is why I moved out here and took up this profession so I wouldn't have to put up with the pressures of the civilized lifestyle.

After a couple of hours of punching the keys my mind runs out of creativity so I push my laptop back and just relax a bit. I keep being startled by noises that normally I don't even notice. Maybe I should bolt the doors tonight. After all, I have a guest and she apparently has more enemies than I do. Besides, I am getting hungry. I get some pork chops out of the freezer and box of au gratin potatoes off the shelf. This will satisfy our hunger if nothing else.

After another half hour I have a meal ready and on the table. I walk over and wake Ginger up. She is so out of it that she comes to the table without any wise remarks. She bows her head when I say grace like she may have some religious training. We eat in silence except for Ginger asking for the salt.

After I finish eating, I go over to my closet and get one of my shirts. I walk over and hand it to Ginger and say, "Here you can wear this for pajamas tonight. You can't keep wearing that towel forever and your own jeans still aren't dry. I know because I just checked them. So put on the shirt and go to bed. You need the rest. After all, we don't need you getting sick and you certainly had a pretty bad chill, you know."

Ginger looks up at me and spits out the words, "Hey Old Man where do you get off telling me what to do."

"Hey yourself Kid. Where do you get off calling me Old Man anyway? I told you my name is John"

"Yeah, you told me your name is John, but Old Man seems to fit better."

At first I am really ticked off, but after a moment it becomes funny having my own words turned back on me. I get a smile on my face as I lower the finger I had raised to shake in her face. "Go on to bed now." I say while turning away and walking to the door. I set the bolt for the first time in I can't remember when. When I turn back around Ginger is standing in the middle of the room wearing the shirt I had given her.

She has a surprised look on her face as she looks up at me and says, "This is a dress shirt. What are you doing with a dress shirt anyway?"

"You know I do get out of the woods once in a while like for business and book signings. I'm not a complete recluse, you know." I say this rather roughly, but the kid may not know that I have any other personality but grumpy. "Now go to bed Kid," I add in a less grumpy voice.

"You want me in the top bunk."

"Nah, go ahead and use the bottom bunk again. I will stay up and keep an eye out for whoever it is that's after you," I say in a rather pleasant manner.

"What, you protect me? You don't even have a gun," she says then she adds the "You know," mocking my habit of using these two words to end my sentences.

"You don't need to be concerned with how I am going to provide protection for you. Just believe me when I say I will do it. Now get to sleep before I put you to sleep Kid." I say putting great emphasis on the word kid.

It doesn't take long after Ginger lies down before she is asleep again. Once about midnight I noticed her tossing and turning and moaning. I walk over and sit down beside her. Suddenly she sits straight up in bed. I grab her by her little shoulders and hold tight. She opened her eyes and says, "I was having a nightmare."

"I know Kid. I know all about nightmares. That's why I don't sleep so well. Now just lay back and think about pleasant things until you fall asleep again. I'll keep watch." All the time I am saying this I am trying to lay her back down, but her little body is so stiff that I am afraid I might hurt her if I apply more pressure.

"After I say I'll keep watch," she relaxes enough that I manage to lay her back down. I stay by her side until I am pretty sure she is asleep again.

CHAPTER 3

THINGS START TO HAPPEN

I walk over to the lower bunk where Ginger is still sleeping soundly. Evidently she had no more nightmares during the rest of the night. I reach down and touch her on the shoulder and say, “Wake up Kid. We have company.”

She opens her eyes and asks, “Who is it?”

“The guy who’s pursuing you, I imagine. Now, I want you to get dressed and put on your coat. When you have that done, I want you to go up in the loft and stay near the loft door. If my plan goes wrong throw the bolt on the door and get out of here as fast as you can. Go uphill and hide for as long as you can. I will join you later, if I am able.”

“You mean if you aren’t dead, right?”

“I am pretty sure my plan will work so get dressed while I watch through a crack between the shutters.” She is on her way to the bathroom to get her clothes on before I make it to the window.

In less than the time I thought it should take her to get dressed I see her scurrying up the steps to the loft. I open the bolt on the door and then ascend the steps to the loft myself.

When I reached the loft Ginger says, "Did you just open the bolt on that door?"

"Yes Kid, I sure did."

"Why did you do that?" she asks," with a note of concern in her voice.

"I did that because, if this is the fellow pursuing you, I want to fight him my way and on my own turf, so just be quiet." I say while reaching over and removing my bow and quiver of arrows from where it's hanging on the wall.

"You have a bow and arrows," the Kids whispers with an astonished look on her face.

"Yes, and I know how to use them, but I don't consider them very effective against a criminal's gun unless I can surprise him. Now, just be quiet so we don't give away the fact that we are here." While I am saying this I look out through one of the observation openings.

"What is that you are looking into," Ginger asks in a whisper.

"It's one of the observation ports I told you about. Then I continue by saying, "be quiet!". The guy is moving towards the cabin."

"Does he have a gun," Ginger asks?

"Yes, and it looks like a semi-automatic so I had better make my first arrow count or we are in a world of hurt. You get back by that door and get ready to run in case something goes wrong.

Ginger does as I request. I notch an arrow into my bow and move to the edge of the loft where I have a complete view of the door our visitor is about to enter.

I hear him climb up the steps to the porch and then walk across the porch. He hesitates at the door for a few moments. I guess he is listening to see if he can hear anything indicating there might be someone inside.

I can feel the adrenaline flowing through my body as though it is being pumped by some giant pumping system. I can't remember having this much of an adrenaline rush since I left Nam.

After a short time I see the door open just a slight bit. Then a hand, holding a pistol extends through the door. I utter a short prayer under my breath asking God to protect us and that the guy I am about to shoot is a criminal and not a rescuer.

Then the door flings wide open and a guy steps through it, fully into the cabin. I pull with my full strength on the bowstring. "Drop the gun and stand still," I tell the intruder. At almost the same moment he turns sharply toward me bringing his pistol around towards me as he turns. This may just be a reaction to the sound of my voice or it may be an attempt to do me harm. I don't wait to see which it is. I loose the bowstring and let the arrow fly. Not too bad a shot actually. The arrow goes through the bicep of his right arm and then into the door pinning him to the door. His pistol goes flying across the room, landing on the floor about mid-room.

The guy lets out a scream that could awaken most of the hibernating bears in our area. Then he spews out a few words not worthy of repeating. I notch another arrow into my bow and pull the string just taut wrapping the index finger, of my left hand, around the bow and the arrow both. This allows me to keep the bow at ready while freeing my right hand for other uses. I descend the steps, move to mid-room and pick up his pistol. "A Glock 45, the favorite of many law enforcement officers. Are you a lawman," I ask?

More four letter words come flying from is mouth followed with a, "I sure am so you had better put down your weapons and get me out of this mess. You're in deep trouble, if you don't know it."

"I really don't believe you about being a lawman. If you are and I am already in trouble, why don't I just give you a little more reason to give me trouble," I say looking him directly in the eye while I am talking. He turns his eyes away from mine almost as soon as our eyes meet. "Now toss me your badge if you have one or toss me your billfold if there is no badge," I say in as intimidating a tone of voice as I can muster up.

Without saying anything he reaches into his inside coat pocket and starts pulling something out. I am relieved beyond words when it turns out to be a billfold and not a badge.

"Get this arrow out of me you idiot," he yells followed by a few more of his seemingly endless list of curse words.

I pay little attention to what he says while continuing to look through his billfold. "I have the feeling from what I am seeing here that you aren't interested in anyone identifying you. I find no driver's license, no credit cards; in fact I find no identification what so ever. However; you have quite an impressive amount of cash in here."

About the time I finish my statement the kid steps into site on the loft. Our unwanted guest sees her and bellowers out. "There you are you little brat. You just wait till I, eh, we get our hands on you. You can't keep getting away from us for long."

"I don't know but it appears to me that she has outsmarted you several times already and it is my true belief that she is enough smarter than you that she can continue doing so. Now, why don't you and I do some trading? I'll pull the arrow out of you arm just as soon as you tell me a very convincing story about how many of you there are up here, where the others are, how you intend to get back together, and any other details you might be able to remember. I advise you not to lie to me. I know ways to detect lies like you have never heard, and then again maybe you know them too. Maybe you were in Nam and have used them too." All the time speaking in the most sinister tone I can muster up.

"I'm alone," he blurts out.

"What about it Kid? Is he telling the truth?"

"No way, there were two of them chasing Mom and I when we left the rest stop"

I look over at a now very frightened looking bad guy and say, "What do you think Kid, would an arrow through his foot improve his memory?" While I am saying this I am walking over to the bow I had left in the middle of the room.

As I pick it up and start reinserting the arrow into the bow our bad man yells out. "Yes there are two of us up here and my friend will be here any minute. You'll be sorry you got yourself involved in our business when he gets here."

"I don't know Mr. Criminal. The kid tells me that there are four of you, all total. You tell me there are two of you. I wonder, which one of you should I believe?"

I have hardly finished my statement when our criminal type fellow starts with a streak of curse words followed by, "The other two went back into town to get some trackers. When they come back they will find you no matter where you go."

"I don't know if that worries me or not. I am having so much fun with you, it might be a lot more fun if there where two of you for me to have more fun. "Now", I say again, using a sinister tone in my voice. "is there anything else that you want to tell me before I finish you off," "No," the would be assassin answers

"Wouldn't you like to tell us where your friend is now and how you were to contact him after you found the kid," I ask trying to keep a glint in my eye like I am enjoying myself.

"We were to meet back at the rest stop," he says, in not too convincing a tone of voice.

"You weren't going to use your cell phone?" I ask.

"No! A cell phone wouldn't even work up here anyway, he says in a voice now starting to quiver.

"Funny thing, I've never had any trouble with mine. Maybe you need to switch to my carrier," I say as I pull my cell from my pocket. "Now give me your cell phone mister and why don't you just quit lying to me? Aren't you even smart enough to notice I can see through every lie you tell.'

Slowly now, the tough guy reaches in his jacket pocket and pulls out his cell phone and hands it to me saying. "Now will you pull his arrow out of my arm? The pain is killing me."

By now the tough guy's voice is sounding rather meek.

I walk over to him and give him a hard punch to the stomach. As he bends in the middle, as much as his arm will allow him to bend, I reach up break the arrow off near his arm and pull his arm off of it. When his arm is free of the arrow he falls in a lump on the floor. He's out like a light.

"What you just did with that guy. Did you learn that in Vietnam?" Ginger asks.

"Nah, Kid, I learned that watching old movies. In Nam we had real interrogators that knew what they were doing. We sure could use one here. I have no idea how much of what he told us is the truth."

Ginger, looking a little frightened of me asks, "Why did you hit him like that?"

"I didn't want him feeling up to hitting me mostly." I tell her as I pick up the intruder by his shoulders and drag him across to the room to a straight chair. "Hey Kid, come over here and hold the chair while I lift this turkey into it. I sure wish this guy had done a little dieting before I had to lift him." For lack of anything better I use some duct tape to affix the legs and arms of our bad guy to the chair.

After I feel that he is secure enough that I can give my attention to other things, I tell Ginger, "We need to get out of here. I have no idea if he had contacted the other fellow, after he found us, or not."

"Why don't you just use your cell phone to call the cops," Ginger asks?"

"It's not that simple Kid. The guy is right. Cell phones don't work up here, at least not in a lot of the area. He wasn't the only one telling lies. I did a little lying too. I'll pack us enough gear for a week or so and we will walk out of here."

"We don't need that much to get out of here, it only took me an afternoon to get here from the rest stop." Ginger says with an air of authority in her voice."

"I know, but the other fellow is in that direction and he may even have help by now, so we need to go the other way out of here. The other way out is up and over the mountain. That will take us as least four days."

Ginger looks me over from head to toe and with a serious look on her face says, "Are you sure you are up to this."

"Sure I am," I answer, "Why do you ask?"

"You're so old. You fought in Vietnam. My mother wasn't even born then. You must be older than my Grandpa and he sure isn't in very good shape."

"Ok, I'll admit that you are right about my age, but I'll make you a deal. I'll quit worrying about you being too young for such a trek if you'll quit worrying about me being too old. Deal?"

"Deal, Old man."

"I just bought a new pack and bed roll. I'll let you carry them. I'll carry my older ones and I'll put most of the load in the old pack. One thing though, we have to do something with that red coat of yours. That thing could be spotted from a mile away in heavy fog.

"What can I do with it? I can't do without it out there, can I?"

"I've got an idea. We will change its color."

Ginger looks at me like I am some kind of a nut, as I hand her a quart of fruit-wood stain and a paint brush. "Now take your coat out on the porch and stain it until no red shows through," I say while making a gesture toward the back door.

While Ginger is outside painting her coat, I pack the backpacks. I pack the one I will be carrying mostly with canned goods and the heavier items. The pack Ginger will be carrying will have the matches, an extra shirt, a pair of pants, some under garments, mess kits, and some candy I found in the cabinet. About the time I am finished packing up our gear Ginger comes back in with her now brown coat.

"Take that thing outside and hang it over the back of the chair on the porch, Kid. We don't need it flaming up from the fire in the fireplace. Gee, that thing smells so strong they may be able to track us by our scent. I sure hope the smell goes away when the stain dries."

Upon finishing rolling our sleeping bags, I slide the backpacks and sleeping bags back behind the table and pull the table cloth down to hide them. We don't need our unwanted guest knowing our plan.

I pick up the first aid kit that I was preparing to put into one of the backpacks and walk over to where our guest is seated. I undo the duct tape holding his right arm to the chair. Slowly I remove his arm from his coat sleeve. I rip his shirtsleeve at the area of the wound. It appears to be a clean wound and is no longer bleeding, at least not much. I put some antibiotic ointment on both sides of his arm at the area of the wound. After this is completed, I wrap a bandage around his arm. The tough guy is conscious now, but doesn't say anything during this entire process.

"You can remove the duct tape from your other arm and you legs yourself," I tell the nameless bad guy.

"I can't. It hurts too much when I move my arm," he says in a tone of voice sounding more like a whiny brat than a real bad guy.
"Then you can stay there if you would rather. I have done everything for you that I intend to." With that comment I step outside to give my attention to Ginger's coat. She has put the stain on much thicker than I had intended but, what the hay, she got the job done. I get a cleaning rag and wipe up the places where her coat has dripped on the floor. I now have a few polka dots on my back porch floor. Oh well, they just blend in with the other stains that have developed over the last several years. I had always intended to use that stain on the floor anyway. That's why I had it here in the first place.

CHAPTER 4

WE RELEASE OUR CAPTIVE AND HIT THE TRAIL OURSELVES

I turn my attention back to our guest. He has now freed himself and is searching his coat pockets. "I took the extra clips for your pistol if that is what you are looking for. I also intend to keep the money you had with you. We will just call it a college fund for the Kid. I don't intend to let you use it to bribe or otherwise influence anyone to do harm to us. Now get out of here"

"I … I can't. I need help. I'll never be able to get out of here on my own," he says in a rather pathetic tone of voice.

"Go on and get out of here. You haven't lost enough blood to be that weak and I sure don't feel too much sympathy for you. After all you came here to kidnap or kill the kid and you wouldn't have hesitated in the least to kill me in the process. I think you're getting a very fair deal from us, all things considered. I would gladly take you to the authorities and turn you in if I weren't afraid we might meet your pals on the way."

Slowly he turns toward the cabin door, walks out of the room, across the porch, down the steps and into the woods. I walk over and close the door after he has disappeared into the woods. I lock and bolt the door, then turning back to the kid. I say, "Grab the pack without the bed rolls on it and follow me."

We exit by way of the back door just in case our would-be assassin or some of his friends might be watching the front of the cabin. I lock the back door and start up the well-worn animal track toward the crest of the mountain. The kid follows me for quite a while before she says a word.

Finally she says, "I can't carry this pack. It is dragging the ground."

I look back and see that she is correct. In my hurry to get on the move I forgot to adjust the pack straps, which were adjusted for my body. "Okay, come on up here and I'll adjust the straps for you."

As I am adjusting the straps to a better fit for her small body she says, "Why are you doing this for me anyway? What's in it for you?"

"Now you tell me, just what am I supposed to do? Am I supposed to let these guys kidnap you or kill you? I must admit there have been a couple of times since I met you that it has been tempting."

"You didn't have to get involved. You could have just not bothered to come out and investigate when you saw me."

"You would have died from exposure by now if you hadn't gotten dry and warm. It doesn't matter anyway. I was involved as soon as you headed toward my cabin. Those guys wouldn't let me live if they even suspected I knew anything about what was going on."

By now I have the straps on the backpack adjusted as short as I can get them, but the pack is more on her backside than her back. We won't be able to travel very fast or very far at a time because the load, as light as I have made it, is quite a chore for the kid's small body. By trying to bring everything we need and still keep the kid's pack light, I have made my pack heavy enough that it is too much of a load for me to carry and make good time anyway.

The animal trail has been created by animals going down to the stream below. As we ascend the mountain, the trail forks often. With each fork the main trail becomes less worn. Sooner or later we will need to leave the main trail and take one of the smaller trails. I don't want to do this too soon though. The more confusing I can make it for anyone following us, the better.

My train of thought is interrupted when the kid grabs my hand and points to something mostly hidden behind an evergreen tree. Without saying a word I move over to investigate. Suddenly I am struck with horror. It is the body of the game warden. This is the first time since I left Nam that I have looked upon a dead body, except at a funeral. I bend down and roll the body over. It's Tom Hanson. I've known him ever since I started building my cabin. He has a bullet hole in his jacket, near his heart. I feel for a pulse, knowing even before I do that there will be none. I hear a noise behind me and turn quickly on the ready to defend myself. It is the kid. Why didn't I think to make her stay on the trail? She didn't need to see this. Finally I stammer out, "I'm sorry you had to see this Kid, Things such as these are the images from which nightmares are made."

Ginger opened her mouth to say something, but nothing comes out. I know the feelings she must be experiencing. I was much older and had received military training before I seen my first victim of a violent death. All these years later, all I have to do is to close my eyes and I can still see that child's face. Now I have let Ginger experience this horror. I take Ginger by the hand and we walk away.

After we have taken only a few steps Ginger give a hard tug to my hand. I look down on her face, which is red from the cold. She says, "Aren't we going to bury him or something. We can't just leave him here like that."

"He is dead. It might have just been a hunter's stray bullet that killed him, but most likely he was killed by the guys looking for you. If this is the case then they are, or at least have been, ahead of us, and they very well may be behind us too. This means we need to keep on the move and keep a close watch in all directions. We'll take the next fork in the trail when we come to it. Maybe this will reduce our chances of walking into one of those guys.

We walk on for some time. It is much further to the next fork than I had expected it to be. By the time we reach it Ginger is lagging well behind. I stop and wait until she catches up to me.

When she reaches me she says, "Can't we stop for a while?

"Sure Kid, but first we need to walk up this branch trail far enough that we won't be noticed from the main trail, then we will rest a while."

Ginger follows me, but her pace has dropped to the point that a snail with the gout could easily pass her up. I find a rather well concealed area off the trail a few yards, drop my pack and go back to the trail for Ginger. I lift the pack off of her small shoulders and sling it over one of my shoulders. It is evident that the Kid is in no condition to keep going. I am starting to worry about her having the strength to climb to the top of the mountain. As mountains go this one is not all that high or steep, never-the-less, it is a mountain.

When we get to the area I had selected for our rest it is evident that Ginger can go no further today. We spread the tarp and lay out the sleeping bags on it. Ginger is shivering again so I suggest she climb into her bedroll. She doesn't say anything she just starts climbing in. I help her remove her coat and then show her how to tuck it in the sleeping bag with her. This will keep the coat warm and help prevent her from getting a chill when she climbs out of the sack. We do the same with her shoes.

I know that Ginger must be completely pooped out because she hasn't made one wise crack since we left the cabin. It is mid-afternoon so we'll just call it a day.

"I am going out and do a little scouting around to see if anyone is following us. I will keep an eye out your way so don't worry about your safety. Just get some rest and try to get warm. Hang in there Kid. I'll be back as soon as I find out what's happening around us.

I pick up my bow and quiver and start moving out using great care to keep as concealed as possible. I haven't moved more that a few dozen yards when I hear a noise on the trail. I freeze and squat down behind what little cover is available to me. I see a guy too well dressed to have planned for a hike in the woods. As he comes closer I notice he is wearing loafers. He is making no effort to look for signs that anyone has been on this trail recently. Also he is not calling out as if they were trying to rescue someone who is lost. All of this leads me to believe he is not a friend. Just as he is passing by my location he trips on an exposed tree root.

He lets out with an oath that sounds just as crude as the oaths of the criminal we held at the cabin this morning. I remain frozen in place until the fellow is well past me before I move out and head back down the trail toward my cabin. Every few yards I hesitate for a few moments to check for sounds of someone else in the area. After doing this, about three or maybe four times I detect that there is someone else in our area. I step off the trail and find concealment. I lay in wait for only a short time when another fellow passes me going up trail. This guy too looks more like a city slicker than a woodsman. This is all I need to know. After this fellow is out of site, I start back toward the site were I had left Ginger.

After only a few yards I hear voices and they sound as though they are approaching me. Again I find concealment and lay low. In only a couple minutes, the two guys I had seen going up the trail appear and are coming back down the trail. I listen to see if I can hear what they are talking about. From a distance it sounds like they are having a disagreement. I gather, from what they say while in earshot, that one of them is going to stay in the cabin tonight. He is to keep watch to see if we try to return. The other fellow is going to go for help.

It is difficult for me to believe, but I do think our friendly hostage lied to us this morning. You just can't trust anyone anymore.

After a few minutes they are out of sight. I wait a few more minutes and then continue back to where Ginger is waiting. When I reach our campsite Ginger is fast asleep. I wake her and explain what I have learned. "I've seen two of our pursuers and managed to overhear enough to know they are calling off their search for the night. They are, however, going to watch the trail so they can catch us if we try to come back down during the night. Tomorrow they are bringing in some locals to join the hunt. It's now close to five in the afternoon. It will be dark soon so it appears that we are safe for now. We don't dare do anything to draw attention in our direction. This means no campfire. I fear it will be a cold, dreary night. I only hope it doesn't become wet also."

I open the pack and get out some canned fruit. The Kid and I share it. When we finish I put the empty can back in the pack, and say, "We will work out a plan in the morning. So get some sleep."

I crawl into my sleeping bag and try to work on a plan for our next move. After a short while I feel myself falling asleep.

Chapter 5

We Face The Facts and Review Our Options.

I awake at just about dawn. The Kid is already awake and addresses me with her usual charm. “I got to go to the bathroom. Where can I go?”

“Here you go. Take the shovel and go over behind that bush. Dig a hole and do your business. When you are finished fill in the hole and camouflage the area with leaves, sticks or whatever you can find. Make it look like the rest of the area around it. If you don’t do a good job you will be leaving a marker for our pursuers.”

Before I can say any more the Kid spews out, “I’m not going to do that. At home we have six bathrooms.”

“Okay Kid, do as you like, but it’s going to be hard to hold it in all day.” With this statement she grabs the shovel and takes off. I didn’t even have time to show her how to unfold and lock it in the straight position. Oh well, she’ll figure it out, I suppose.

When Ginger gets back she hands me the shovel. I have rolled up the sleeping bags and tied them on the back of one of the packs. I look down at Ginger and say, "Okay Kid it was evident that we were both overloaded yesterday so I will carry both packs today."

Before I can finish what I am saying Ginger lashes out at me saying, "You just do your share Old Man and I'll handle my share"

I just shake my head and take off walking. This Kid is harder to be nice to than a rabid skunk. When we get back to the animal trail I turn uphill. I figure we have about three or four hours before the hoods can get locals out here and organized into a party to track us. Going will be slower for them than for us because they'll have to be tracking us.

The trail is now running almost straight uphill. The going is tough, but we need to keep on going as long as we can. We will need to stop and eat around noon.

After about an hour has passed Ginger has fallen well behind me. I stop and wait until she catches up. When she gets up to me she says, with all the charm of a rattlesnake, "Hey Old Man why are we doing all of this climbing anyway. Why don't we just pick a good spot to hide and then shoot them when they show up? You have that guy's gun and your bow and arrows so it wouldn't be too hard to do."

"Kid, I'm not about to shoot anybody. Just get that through your head, will you?"

"Why not Old Man," she says emphasizing the Old Man in revenge for my having call her Kid. "I bet you killed a plenty in Vietnam Didn't you?"

"Yea Kid, you're right about that. Enough to learn that killing isn't the answer to anything. Killing just begets more killing and the killing just goes on and on.

"I suppose you have a better idea then, huh Old Man."

"Give me a break Kid. I'm doing the best I can here. This is nothing like Vietnam. In Vietnam I was with soldiers, not a kid. I had orders to follow. I had equipment designed to do the job we were there to do. We had a known enemy even though we couldn't always identify them. Things there and then were nothing like things are here and now."

"We should have stayed at the cabin. We could have had some protection there and we wouldn't be cold and tired like we are now doing this your way."

"Yeah sure, until they burned the cabin with us in it. Just what did your Dad do to make these guys so mad anyway?"

"I don't know what he did to get anyone so up tight. He was a pilot. He had his own plane and his own company. Mom said he flew precious cargo whatever that means." Like I told you before, he didn't hang much at home."

"Come on, we have to keep moving. By now I figure the locals are organized and are starting to trail us."

The Kid mutters something. I didn't hear what she said, but I'm most likely better off that I didn't. The trail we are following is now veering slightly on an angle from a direct path to the mountain peak. This is good. I don't think either one of us could stand to stay on that steep a climb for too much longer. It is almost noon now, so I think we need to eat. I look back down the trail. The kid is back about twenty yards, sitting down on the trail. I walk back down to where she is sitting and ask, "What's the matter?"

"What do you think is the matter? I'm pooped, that's, what's the matter."

"Okay then, we will stop for lunch and rest a bit," I say with a slight sound of sympathy in my voice. Actually, I know just what she is feeling. I am tired, as well, and sore all over.

I reach into my pack and pull out a couple of sticks of beef jerky. I hand a piece to the kid. She looks at it like it is something that came from outer space. "Just bite off a piece and chew on it." She slowly puts it in her mouth and bites down on it. After several pulls she manages to tear off a piece. From the look on her face it is evident that she is not fond of beef jerky. "I know, Jerky doesn't taste like steak, but it is about all we have to eat and it is definitely all we have time to eat right now.

I glance down the path and notice that we are leaving a trail a blind man could follow. We need to do better at concealing our trail or our pursuers will catch up with us in another day or two at the most. The trails are damp enough that we can't walk on them without leaving footprints. If we walk off the trails we will leave evidence in the way of broken twigs on bushes and disturbed leaves and plants on the ground.

I walk back to where the kid is still chewing on the jerky. "Okay Kid, we have a problem. We are leaving a trail so plain that even those city slickers can follow us. We need to figure a way to fool the trackers at least for a while. So far I haven't come up with much of an idea on how we can do this. If we could figure out how to not leave a trail, even for a while would help. Do you have any ideas Kid?"

"Yeah, if only we could fly." the kid says with her usual sarcastic attitude.

"Hey, you may just have the answer there."

"Now you aren't going to tell me you know how to fly are you."

I'll do better than that. I'll even teach you how to fly. We need to find just the right tree at just the right distance from the trail. We also need to leave lots of footprints on the trail. Just maybe, we can fool them long enough for us to get a better advantage in the distance between us and them. Come on grab your pack and follow me. We need to walk back and forth a few times to confuse our trackers as to where we left the trail. You can chew on your jerky while we are walking."

"You know Old Man, it didn't take me long to decide that you are a little touched in your head, but now I believe you are totally around the bend. Teach me to fly you say ——-?"

The kid never finishes her sentence. She just picks up her pack and follows me. About twenty yards back down the trail I find a tree that looks like it just might be what we are looking for. The fork branching off the trunk is a little lower than I had hoped for, but the ground drops off rather steeply so it just may work anyway. I look back up the trail and see that the kid will catch up with me soon. I move around to check where the best angle for throwing the rope between the trunk and the limb's fork might be. As the kid catches up to me and stops, I motion for her to hand me her pack. I open it and pull out the rope I had brought. It is pretty lightweight for swinging on, but with any luck it will hold. I had brought it to use pulling the packs up a grade that was too steep for us to carry them. At least it is a new rope so it shouldn't have any weak or worn spots.

I find a stick that looks like it might make a good weight for the end of the rope. It is about two inches in diameter and three feet long. It seems to be sturdy enough. I tie it to the end of the rope and then unfurl the remainder of the coil. Sometimes a guy gets lucky. On my second toss the stick goes cleanly between the trunk and the fork. I slowly pull the slack out of the rope and the stick wedges in the fork of the limb, just as I had planned.

The kid looks up at me and says, "You've gotta be kidding Old Man. There's no way I'm going to go flying down that hill hanging from a rope. You go right ahead and kill yourself if you want, but I don't want to be any part of your death wish."

I pick up my pack first and give it a heave down the hill toward the tree. This time I'm not so lucky. It goes flying by the tree and lands in some brush about twenty feet past the tree. I pick up the kid's pack and give it a toss. It lands a little closer to target than my pack had, but still isn't on target by any means. I look down at the kid and say, "Alright once this rope swings downhill there isn't much of a way to get it back up so we are going to go together. When I say ready I want you to grab me around the waist and hold on as tight as you can. Okay?" She just nods and looks like she is going to be sick.

I find another stick and loop the rope around it, two or three times, at about the extent of my reach. This will help me hold the rope and may prevent me from getting rope burns on my hands.

"Okay Kid, grab me around my waist."

She comes up behind me and grabs hold. "No, grab from the front. That way if the rope breaks I won't fall on top of you." She does as I suggest without comment. She must be scared. Otherwise she would have made some wise crack about my hair-brained idea.

I grab a firm grip on the stick and raise my feet. We go swinging out and well past the tree. I wait until we swing back closer to the tree and then straighten my knees. My feet don't hit the ground. We are suspended with my feet about four feet from the ground. Oh well, there is nothing to do but to let go. I try to land like we were taught to land when we jumped from helicopters in Vietnam. When we land my knees buckle like they are supposed to but they don't stop buckling. I go down and, to make things worse, the kid is under me. If she had held on from my back, like she started to, I wouldn't have landed on top of her. She is quick to point his out to me once I manage to get up.

All and all this has been a rather successful venture. I allow the weight of the stick, which is wedged between the limbs' fork, to pull the rope down. I coil it up and put it over my shoulder. "Come on, let's go get our packs and get out of here. Hopefully, there is enough distance between the trail we left and where we start to leave a new trail, the trackers will have a hard time making the connection."

The kid grabs her pack and puts it on. She looks up at me and says, "We are downhill of where we were. I thought you said we should keep going uphill."

"Yeah I know. I just hope that by reversing our direction we will fool those trackers for a little longer. Also you can't very well swing uphill on a rope, you know."

Chapter 6

The Rains Come

We walk in a straight line going neither, uphill or downhill. After walking for an hour or so we are both too pooped to continue. It is much more difficult picking our way through the underbrush than it was walking on the trail. I start looking for a good place to set up camp for the night when I feel the first drop of rain.

"Okay Kid, this isn't a very good place for a campsite, but it is going to have to do. We don't dare let your clothes get wet since we don't have any extra clothes for you."

One thing about walking off the trail, Ginger can keep up with me much better. Her small body fits through the opening in the brush much better than my much larger body. While this thought is running through my head I spot an outcropping of rock which will at least keep the water, running down the mountain, from running directly over us. I point to it and Ginger starts toward it without my having to say a word. As soon as we reach it, I remove my pack and start spreading the tarp. Then I lay out the sleeping bags Ginger takes the hint and removes her jacket. She crawls inside her sleeping bag pulling the jacket and shoes inside after her.

It rains gently for about an hour and then quits. After the rain is over, I push open the rain flap on my sleeping bag. A short time later Ginger does the same.

Her eyes are red and dewy. It appears she has been crying. "What's the matter Kid," I ask.

Much too crusty to admit to such a human emotion as crying she merely says, "Do you think they've gotten my mother."

"I have no way of knowing whether they have caught her or not. I do know this much though, if your mother is as tough and wily as you, I'd bet she's doing just fine."

Then she says, "Oh well, my mother isn't much of a mother either. She's always working, away on business or entertaining a client. She's never around too much. Dad was always staying in the city during the week and Mom off, during her thing. I feel closer to the staff than I do my family."

"It sounds to me like your mother risked her life trying to get your pursuers to follow her so you could escape. That seems to me like she had a lot of love for you Kid, whether you aware of it or not"

Ginger gets a look of astonishment on her face which soon turns to a look of fear. Not fear of her pursuers, but a fear of having lost her mother without ever having taken the time to tell her just how much she loved her. At least that is my guess of what is running around in that little mind of hers.

When she regains her composure she asks, "Where do your daughters live?"

"I have absolutely no idea where they are, what they are doing, or anything else about them. I lost track of them years ago."

"Don't you want to know?" Ginger asks with a note of concern in her voice, which is an attitude I have not observed in her personality before.

"Sure I do, but by the time I got sobered up and had my life back on track it was too late. Their mother had divorced me and was remarried. I heard, from some of our mutual friends, that she married a real nice guy who was being a fine step-dad to my daughters. At first I wrote to them a few times, but I never got an answer. I can understand that though. About all they could possibly remember of me was a drunken, loud mouthed, abusive, guy."

"What made you that way? Was it Vietnam?"

"Yeah, I guess so Kid. At least, I wasn't that way before I went to Nam."

"What were you like before that?"

"I guess I was just a pretty average guy. I met my wife while I was in my sophomore year of college. She and I met in the student union. She was with a group of my friends having a Coke between classes. I liked what I saw so the next time we met I asked her for a date. We started dating quite a bit. We were married in my senior year. After I graduated, I took a job teaching and Linda finished her degree."

"You are a teacher?" Ginger says with an air of disbelief in her voice.

"Yeah Kid, I was a teacher. Even harder to believe I was an English teacher. You sure can't tell that by the way I talk now can you?"

Ginger doesn't answer my question, but just looks at me with a curious look, so I continue telling her about me. "Linda became pregnant shortly after her graduation and Kelly was born the next February. I was drafted shortly after Kelly was born. While I was home on leave after basic training Linda became pregnant again. Anglia was born after I was in Nam."

After a long period of silence Ginger says, "Well don't just stop there. Tell me what turned the school teacher into a sot?"

"You have a nice way with words too, Kid," I say before continuing. "When I came back from Nam I was plagued with nightmares. Every night was the same. It got to where the last thing I wanted to do was go to sleep. I stayed up to all hours, but sooner or later the body's need for sleep is going to win out. One of my buddies told me that drinking helped. He said when he was drunk he could sleep for several hours before the nightmares came. I tried it. It may have worked for him, but it didn't work for me. To say the least, my wife tried. She tried to get me to tell her about Vietnam. She said maybe it would help if I told someone about it."

"Did you tell her about it?"

"How could I tell her about what happened in Vietnam? That was what was causing me to have nightmares. I didn't want to give her nightmares too. It was bad enough that I was stuck having them I didn't need to cause her to have them as well, so I just re-enlisted and volunteered for another tour in Nam."

Ginger gets a curious look on her face and asks, "Now what would you do that for? Isn't that what caused you your problem in the first place?"

"There is no way I can explain this to you. I don't even think I understand it myself."

"Was it because of your wife?"

"No, I give my wife or rather my ex-wife no blame what-so-ever for my problems. She did everything anyone could be expected to do and then some. It was that no one understood. Half of the people considered me a hero and wanted to buy me a drink to celebrate what I had done in Nam. The other half called me names like baby killer, war monger, and so on."

"Were some of the solders baby killers and war mongers," Ginger asks?

"No. At least they didn't start out that way. They were just guys like you would meet on any street in America. No better, no worse. At least they were no better or worse than the average guy until they had seen too much."

"Too much of what?"

"I'll tell you what there has been too much of Kid. There's been too much talk. I've already told you more than I've told anyone else since I came back from Nam. The next thing I know you will be having nightmares too." With this I scoot down in my sleeping bag and close my eyes.

I lay there thinking for a while. Actually, I have mostly overcome the nightmares and other problems resulting from being in Nam. If I hadn't, I don't think I would still be alive. Either that or I would have gone completely mad, long ago. I wonder if the Kid doesn't think maybe I am at least about half-mad now. It must be tough having to rely on someone you don't know and totally don't understand. This is the last thing I remember. I must have fallen asleep while having those thoughts.

Upon waking it dawns on me that all we had to eat all day yesterday was that beef jerky we chewed on while we were walking. It is cold, everything is damp and it will be slippery walking, but my biggest problem right now is withdrawal from coffee. Just as I am about to unzip my sleeping bag, so I can get out of it, I hear something. The hair on the back of my neck feels like it is standing straight out. I lay perfectly still afraid to move a muscle for fear of being found. Laying flat on my back with my bow and arrows about four feet away makes me pretty vulnerable. I have the pistol I took from the fellow, but I fear using it might attract attention by everyone looking for us. I strain to hear if there are any further noises. The next noise I hear is a sound like someone moving on the trail above us. After a few more seconds, that seems much longer, I can make out voices. At first I can't tell much of what is being said but, as they move closer, I hear enough to make me very concerned about our safety.

The first voice I hear says, "Did you find anything?"

"No. I've walked well past the place where their tracks ended and I found nothing else. Did you find anything?

"No. I have searched both sides of the trail back well beyond where they had walked up and down the trail several times and I found no place where they left the trail."

"Well they can't have just disappeared. They had to go somewhere."

"Do you think they were picked up by a helicopter?"

"No, I don't, for several reasons. First a helicopter couldn't get in here. Second a helicopter couldn't even drop a line into this densely a forested an area. Third if a chopper came in here to pick them up there is no way we wouldn't have heard it. So what I think most is it's a dumb question for you to ask."

"Dumb it may be, but do you have a better idea of how they could just disappear like that."

"Yeah, I think I do. I think they swung out of here like Tarzan. Only problem with that idea is there aren't any vines around here, but I will bet they are below us. It's for sure they couldn't have swung uphill."

"What do you suggest we do?"

"I'm going to keep going up the trail to see if they may have come back up and gotten back on the trail above us. I want you to go back down to where this fork branched off to see if they tried to backtrack and cross behind us. I'll give Jerry a call on the radio and tell him to watch the branch trail below to be sure they don't go down. Now get going."

I can hear both of these guys heading off, one going up the trail and one going down the trail. I wait until I feel they are well out of earshot and then turnover to wake up the kid, but I find her wide-awake, with a look of near panic on her face.

"I guess you heard what they were saying?"

"What are we going to do now?

"Good question. Somehow we have to get out of this box we have ourselves in. I fear that I grossly underestimated how good these trackers would be. The first thing we need to do is to get our sleeping bags packed up so we can get out of here."

All the time we are packing up I'm trying to formulate a plan in my head. I seem to be able to formulate all kinds of ways to get us killed, but I am having a little trouble coming up with a plan to save us. Then a bright idea pops into my head. The trouble with this idea is I can't figure out if it will save us or get us killed.

"Okay Kid here's the plan. I have learned from experience that trackers are just that, trackers. They keep their heads down looking for tracks. So since they don't look up we are going to get above them and just let them track themselves right past us."

Before I can say any more the kid butts in. "Where did you learn that, in Vietnam?"

"No, I learned that playing hide and seek with my cousin. I climbed up in a tree and she spent an hour looking for me. She must have walked under me ten times during that hour without once looking up."

"Was she a tracker?"

"No, but she was a pretty savvy farm girl. Now, here is what we are going to do. We will walk in a wide circle and then join back up with the trail we made getting here. Since the trackers can't tell how many times we have walked a trail in the woods, like they can on the animal trail, they will think we are heading back to the upper animal trail when actually, after we get to where the new trail joins with the old trail, we will turn back and back-track to a tree I will have picked out. Then we will climb up in the tree. All we have to do then is to wait there and let them pass under us."

"This plan sounds pretty stupid to me," Ginger says with the usual sound of sarcasm in her voice and as usual I just ignore her and go on with my plan.

We start walking in a wide circle. All the time we are walking I am looking for a climbing friendly tree. I have no idea how good the kid can climb, but I do know that her legs are short and won't reach from one limb to another limb if the limbs are very far apart. We have walked what I would estimate to be half way around the circle when my eye catches sight of something up in a tree. Then it dawns on me. My buddy, Jack, and I built that thing several years ago. It looks down over a small stream where animals drink. I kind of survey to see how much of an angle one has to raise his head to see it. It is not as veiled as I would like it to be, but it will have to do because I don't seem to be finding anything better. I need to widen the arc of our trail a little so we will walk within easy reach of its limbs without leaving evidence that this tree is any different than the hundreds of others we've walked past.

After satisfactorily modifying the arc and walking by the tree stand, we continue walking until we complete the circle and end up back where we started. The Kid looks up at me and says, "Hey old man, I'm pooped. Can't we rest for a few minutes?"

"Kid, if we rest now we may be having eternal rest soon. I have no idea how far those trackers are behind us and we are going to be walking back toward them now. Do you think you can last another thirty minutes before we rest."

"Yea, when you put it that way I guess I'd better be able to do it."

With this, we turn and start walking back toward the tree with the stand built in it. When we reach it I help Ginger remove her backpack. Then I lift her up and sit her on the lowest limb. I remove my pack and take out the rope and slip it through the straps of both packs. After affixing it securely, I coil the remainder of the rope except for a length long enough to reach Ginger. "Okay Kid, do you think you can catch this if I throw it up to you?"

"If you can get up to me Old Man, I can catch it," she says with a note of mockery in her voice.

To my surprise she catches it on my first throw even though my throw is not a good one. Now it is up to me to get myself up in the tree. I grab the limb on the trunk side of Ginger and pull my legs up and wrap them around the limb. This isn't too hard, but I have quite a struggle getting myself from this position to the sitting position. Ginger gets a kick out of watching my struggles. I take the rope from Ginger and loop it over the next limb up then I lift Ginger up and set her on it. Thankfully, this limb and most of the rest of the limbs up to the stand are spaced such that I can just step up from one to the other. After I climb up to each new limb I reach down and take Ginger by the hands and pull her up too. We repeat this process until we are atop the stand itself. It has been several years since Jack and I built this thing, but it is in surprisingly good condition.

I take the rope from around my shoulder and start pulling the packs up. Of course, about half way up they turn in a direction such that the sleeping bags won't pass between two limbs. After numerous tries to get it to spin into a position where it will pass between the two limbs I finally surrender. I tie the rope off on a limb above the stand and climb down to where I can adjust the packs so the sleeping bags will pass between the two limbs. When I reach them I find that the pack has already spun into the proper position to pass easily between the two limbs. I hear the kid giggling. Sometimes I almost understand why someone would want to do her in.

Finally the packs, sleeping bags, Ginger and I all are on the stand. The problem is there's no room for all of this stuff. I pull the sleeping bags and my bow and quiver off the backpacks. I suspend the backpacks from a limb so they are hanging beside the stand. Then we spread out the sleeping bags. We are starting to feel the cold now that we are no longer walking. The exercise of walking and climbing helped keep us warm, but now that we are just sitting we are cold. We crawl into the sleeping bags, but don't zip them up. We remain in a sitting position leaning back against the tree trunk.

I reach over and pull a can of kippered herring, some crackers and a couple of bottles of water from the backpack and say, "I think we had better eat something. If we don't keep up our strength we can't keep on going."

"I'm not hungry, so I'll just pass on the eating bit."

"Ah come on Kid. You are going to love this stuff. It's a delicacy," I say while pulling the tab to open the can.

Once the aroma of the herring reaches the Kid's nostrils she makes a face and says, "You aren't really going to eat that stuff are you? It smells like it was dead for a long time before they canned it."

I pay no attention to her complaints. I just spread a little of the herring on a cracker and tell her, "eat."

To my surprise she just pinches her nose between her left fore finger and thumb. She takes the cracker out of my hand and stuffs it in her mouth. Then she chews a couple of times and swallows it almost whole.

I watch her face for a few seconds and see her expression change. "You know, you're right. That stuff isn't half-bad. Give me another one."

"You know, I think that's a first for you. If I'm not mistaken that is the first time you have admitted that I was right about anything."

"Maybe so, but you were right one time before"

"Just once? Pray tell me when that was Kid?

"When you told me I was going to catch my death of a cold if I didn't come in out of the rain. You know, when you found me hiding from you."

"Well, it is good to know that I have been right twice now, and in only three days. I think that betters my average."

CHAPTER 7

THE KID PSYCHOANALYZES ME

We complete our tin of kippered herring and also eat a can of fruit cocktail without any further conversation. Finally the kid says, "Do you think we will be able to see the campfires when our pursuers make camp for the night."

"No, I expect they have MRE's. They came prepared to camp out. I doubt that they will even use sternos."

I notice how the sky appears and say, "I sure hope it doesn't rain. I had enough of being out in the rain in Nam."

"Tell me Old Man, if you hated it so much in Nam why did you go back? You told me you did a couple of tours there didn't you?"

"How old are you anyway Kid?"

"I'm older than you think I am, Old Man," She says with great emphasis on the old man part.

"Why do you have such an interest in the Vietnam conflict anyway? Like you said, 'that war was over before your Mother was born'."

"I find myself very dependent on one of the relics of that era so I am just trying to find out something about what I am depending on" she says.

"Well, how am I doing so far?"

"Not too well, as best as I as can tell. So far you have gotten us stuck out in the woods with our pursuers on both sides of us. We are not too well off in the way of provisions and you say you aren't willing to kill anyone. That doesn't make me feel too protected."

"Then why are you sticking with me?"

"If I wasn't with you I would already be dead, that's why. Now are you going to answer my question or not?"

"I told you once before that no one at home understood how things were. I got tired of people wanting to buy me drinks to celebrate the job we were doing over there and I got even more tired of people calling me baby killer. I started avoiding people as much as I could. Finally, one day, I decided to visit my friend Tom's dad. Tom had been killed in Nam. After we talked for a while, mostly about Tom and I during our high school days. Tom's dad handed me a letter he had received. When I read the letter I couldn't believe anyone would be cruel enough to write something like that. It said that the writer was glad that Tom was dead. It said that his death had removed one more baby killer from this earth. I couldn't finish reading it. It lit a blaze of anger in me such as I had never known in my life. It was plain to me that I no longer belonged in this society so split over an issue that really seemed to have little to do with what was going on in Vietnam. I realized that the only place I could find others who understood what I was going through was back in Nam. It was the only place where I could be with others who realized people were dying, or being mutilated both physically and mentally. Those effects would last for the rest of their lives. All of this for a cause that our government said was important, but one that the American public no longer was willing to support."

"Did going back help?"

"It did while I was there, but all conflicts come to an end. When I came back, things had changed but not for the better as far as we veterans from Nam were concerned. I still didn't feel that I fit in with society. In fact, I still don't fit in anywhere Kid."

"Were you really a baby killer?"

"Kid, the enemy would go into villages and then fire upon us. We fired back. Village people were killed. Some were babies. If we hadn't fired back they would have killed us. Now that is how it was and from now on we talk no more about Nam. Okay?"

"Okay Old Man, if that's the way you want it.

This kid makes me mad even when she is agreeing with me. I guess I'm not mad at the Kid. It's more that I am mad after thinking of the injustice of that whole fiasco. I feel that if we weren't going to stay until the mission we started was complete then we should never have been there in the first place. So many good soldiers died. So many civilians were killed and maimed. So many lives were messed up with memories that destroy from within.

Both the Kid and I sit in silence, each lost in our own thoughts for some time. Finally the kid breaks the silence by saying, "Hey Old Man, you aren't still doing that drinking stuff are you?"

"No I gave that up a long time ago."

The Kid says nothing more for quite some time, but you can almost see the wheels turning in that little head of hers. Finally she asks the question that had been running around in her pretty little head.

"How did you do that?"

"Do what Kid?"

"Like give up drinking."

"I woke up one morning to find myself laying face up on the sidewalk. A little girl was standing there looking down on me. My hand was cut from a broken bottle. I guess it broke when I fell. If it had been only a few degrees colder I wouldn't have awakened at all. I was filthy. I stunk. I smelled of booze, sweat, body odor and heaven knows what else. At first I thought the little girl was my daughter. The thought of my daughter seeing me like this was almost more than I could bear. Of course it was not my daughter and the little girl's mother ran over and took her by the hand and led her away from the dirty old man. That's what did it for me. I picked myself up and walked to the nearest Salvation Army shelter. There I found the help I needed to cast out my demons and to climb my way back up from the abyss I had sunken into. It took quite a while, but I got a job working as a custodian."

"A custodian, isn't that a janitor," the Kid says with a look of disbelief on her face. "Why would you do that? Didn't you tell me you were a school teacher? Why didn't you just go back to teaching?"

"There's nothing wrong with being a janitor Kid. It's honest work. Besides I had not kept my credentials up so I could teach. I would have needed to go back to school and I sure didn't have the money for that."

"What about your family? Couldn't you have gotten some help from them?"

"By that time I had been on the streets for over twenty-five years. My parents had been killed in an auto accident and my brother couldn't even find me to let me know." I did go back home after I got my life back together, but there were strangers living in the home place. They didn't know who I was. By then my brother had been transferred by his company and no longer lived in our home-town. Later on I found him and we have kept in touch ever since."

"How did you get started writing anyway?"

"One of the buildings I cleaned was a publishing company. I got to know one of the staff. She quite often worked late, as did many of them. One night she made mention that I spoke like a schoolteacher. I told her that might be because I had been one. Over time I told her several things about my life. One evening she suggested that I should write a book about my life. She said it might help others to understand the homeless better. After thinking about it for some time I decided to do it. I couldn't afford anything more than a pencil and notebooks so I wrote it all in long hand. After I finished it I didn't have the courage to give it to anyone."

"Why not, like what were you afraid of anyway?"

"Failure Kid. I was afraid of failing again. What if they didn't like it? What if it wasn't any good? I wasn't sure that I could take failing again. I was, by now, being a success, even if it was only at being a janitor."

"Did it ever get published?"

"Yes, it did. I carried it to work with me every evening thinking I would show it to Kathy, but my courage would fail me before I could give it to her. One evening she saw me when I came in and asked me if this was my book. I lied. I told her it was just a rough draft of what I intended to write. She said she would like to read it. She said maybe she could be of some help since she was an editor. Reluctantly, I gave her the notebook. The next evening when I came in she broke the news to me that she had shown it to her boss and he wanted to publish it and they did."

"Are you still writing?"

"Yes, I am still writing. What is it with all these questions anyway? Are you going to write a book?"

"No. Somehow I don't think a book about you would be too interesting. I am just trying to find out who I am with is all."

After another long silence the kid asks, "Where are you from anyway? You sure don't talk like you are from here."

"You're right about that. I grew up in Perry Oklahoma and lived most of my adult life in Oklahoma City."

"Why did you move up here anyway? Don't you want to be near your home?"

"Most of my family is gone from that area now. I guess I just needed to get away from the places where I did my drinking and the friends I did my drinking with so I got on a bus going northeast and here is where I got off."

Ginger sits for quite some time with a serious look on her face. Finally she says, "You could have picked a better place you know."

"Most likely so but, it is starting to get dark so let's try to get some sleep." With this last statement I slipped down into my sleeping bag and closed my eyes. I kept thinking of what the Kid said about wanting to know who she was with. I am sure her parents have warned her about going with strangers and now her only choice is to go with me, a total stranger. No wonder she is so curious about me. I am sure she finds me a very strange stranger at that. I can't help wondering about her too. She appears to be maybe ten or eleven years old, but she talks like a college graduate. She is slight of build, but appears to be as tough as ten penny nail. She talks like she cares for no one, yet I feel she has deep feelings. To say the least she is a strange kid. Who knows, maybe we deserve each other.

Chapter 8

The Oppositions Makes a Mistake

I awake this morning to the sound of voices not too distant from our location. As I listen for a while it is plain that the voices are coming nearer. I lay as still as I possibly can, hoping to do nothing that might attract the attention of the people moving toward us. I sure hope what I told Ginger about trackers is correct. If they look up they can't possibly miss seeing the blind that we are on. Finally the trackers move in close enough that I can make out what they are saying. It would be nice if they would outline their strategy, but I guess this is wishful thinking. After what seems like hours, but in reality it wasn't nearly that long, they walk under us. The only thing I hear, while they are within earshot that might be of use to us, is that they are following the trail we left hoping they would follow.

When the trackers are far enough away I turn to wake up Ginger only to find her laying stiff as a board with eyes the size of pomegranates. She speaks first whispering, "Are they gone?"

"I think they are. At least I can't see or hear them anymore."

"What do we do now?"

"Okay, as soon as these guys get far enough away that they aren't likely to hear or see us, we are going to get down from here and hightail it back down the mountain. Since they came up through the woods and not on a trail, we will be able to follow the track they made coming up. That will make it difficult for them to track us."

"Don't you think there will be some of them at your cabin waiting for us to do just that," the Kid asks with a tone of authority in her voice.

"Yes I do and that is just exactly why we aren't going back to the cabin. We are going down to where I garage my car. If they aren't there we will drive out of here and get some help."

"And what if they are there? What will we do then?"

"Hey, I don't have all the answers, you know. We will just do what we think is best at the time."

Yeah, I am very aware that you don't have all the answers, you know.

"Well I do know one answer. We need to get out of here and we need to do it now."

All the while we have been talking I have been rolling up the sleeping bags and repacking our packs. Using the rope, I lower everything to the ground except the Kid and myself. I help the Kid down the same way I helped her to get up, one limb at a time. Once we are on the ground I hand the Kid the lightest pack and then take off down the path the locals made coming up. After only a few dozen steps I glance back to see Ginger lagging well behind while struggling to carry the pack. Her slight little body is just not able to handle much of a load. I turn and walk back toward her. When we meet I lift the pack off of her back and remove a few items that we may need. After placing the items I had removed from her pack into my pack, I hide her pack in a bush.

Of course as soon as Ginger figures out what I am doing, she puts her mouth into gear and starts protesting.

"Hey Old Man, I can carry my own weight. You don't have to do favors for me."

"I'm not doing you a favor Kid. I am doing me a favor. I want to get out of here as fast as I can. So just button your lip and try to keep up with me. Okay?"

"Okay Old Man. Just make sure to stay out of my way or I just very well may pass you up. Okay?"

I start to say something, but remember before I do that this will only bring on another statement from the Kid. She always has to get in the last word. So I just start walking back down the trail toward the garage where I keep my car stored. I hope the thugs haven't found it, but if they have I will figure out some way to get us out of here in spite of them. If my bearings are correct we should reach it by mid-afternoon. The kid is right about one thing though. Now that she isn't carrying that fool pack she is about to step into my footprints before I make them.

Neither Ginger nor I say anything for the next hour or so, but I have the feeling that that little mind of hers is busy again. Sure enough I have no more than finished this thought and her mouth flies open.

"Hey Old Man, I'm hungry. You have anymore of that chewy beef stuff."

The kid is right. It is well past noon and now that she has brought it up, I am hungry too. She is right in another way too. We need to keep moving so we should eat on the go. "Sure Kid I'll grab us each a chunk of jerky," I say, stopping and removing my pack.

After getting each of us a hunk of jerky, I close the pack and sling it back over my shoulders. Again we walk for a couple of hours without saying anything. This time I break the long silence. "You sit down and wait here for a few minutes. If I am not mistaken the garage should be just a little way south of here. I'll go down and scope it out then come back for you. You just hide over there by that bush and make yourself invisible. Okay?"

"Okay Old Man. You just make sure you don't get yourself into any trouble without me there to bail you out. You're pretty old to be out on your own, you know."

"Okay, I'll keep that in mind," I say as I turn away from the trail, going downhill and turn south toward the area where I think my garage is located.

Before I have walked more that a few minutes the garage comes into view. Since I can now see the garage it is reasonable to assume that anyone in that area can see me too. I kneel down and remove the pack. I then remove my bow from my shoulder and pull an arrow from the quiver. I try to move with as much stealth as I can, but it is difficult to move silently in the woods with twigs snapping and leaves rustling under your feet, to say nothing about the exposed tree roots that keep tripping me. I stand behind the trunk of a large, old tree and peer around it to see if there is any sign of someone being nearby. After several minutes of observation I spot something moving. It is a shadow of a man. I freeze and wait to see if he will move far enough to come into my view. After what seems like an eternity he finally moves into view. I am relieved to see it is our old friend from the cabin. His arm is in a sling and the only thing I see in his hand is a walkie-talkie. After a few minutes he walks out of sight again. As soon as I feel he is not returning to my view I take off back toward the kid.

When I get back to where I had left Ginger, my heart sinks. She is nowhere in sight. Just as I am about to panic I hear her mouthing off behind me.

"I did a pretty good job of making myself invisible didn't I Old Man?"

"Yeah, you sure did Kid. Good enough to give me a near heart attack."

Did you find the garage? Was there anybody there? Do you have a plan for getting us to your car?

"Wait a minute. One question at a time, please! I did find the garage. The idiot we captured at the cabin is guarding it. He has a radio and is most likely in contact with the others. Finally, I am working on a plan. Let's just pray that it works.

"You sure pray a lot. I've seen you do it several times. You're not one of those Jesus freaks my Mom told me about are you?"

"Well, that's not exactly how I would refer to myself Kid, but I am a Christian if that is what you mean. Now let's move out. I'll pray on the move since we need to get to the car and out of here before dark. We'll talk more about Christianity later, if we live long enough. Okay?"

"Okay."

"Now I'll take short steps. You step only where I have stepped. If I give you a hands down signal you kneel as fast as you can."

After giving these instructions I move out toward the garage. Considering everything we make pretty good time and in a few minutes we are back to the friendly old tree that hid me before. The local idiot is nowhere to be seen. I give a hands down signal to Ginger and then move out to see if I can find him.

After I move far enough to see the south side of the garage I observe as beautiful a site as I have ever seen. There sitting on a rock near the garage and leaning back against the garage is our adversary. He is asleep. Slowly I creep down to the level of the garage. This fellow must be a pretty sound sleeper because I can't say that my trek was silent, but he never moved a muscle. I don't have time to deal with this guy too long so I pick up a softball size rock and bring it down on his head. Needless to say he never woke up. In fact I doubt that he will wake up for some time. The best part is he never even had time to key his radio. I step back to where Ginger can see me and motion for her to come on down.

"What did you do that fellow anyway," Ginger asks when she sees his prostrate body lying on the ground.

"I gave him a sleeping potion. I don't think he is going to wake up for some time now," I say as I am examining him to be sure I haven't killed him. He is still breathing and is not bleeding too profusely so I guess he will live. I motion for Ginger to follow me and we walk around to the front of the garage. I unlock the garage door and open it. I am half surprised to see my car sitting there, apparently in good order. The proof of the pudding will be to see if it will start or if they had the good sense to disable it. To my surprise it starts. I throw the pack and my bow and arrows into the back seat, at the same time motioning for Ginger to get in. I open the trunk. Then I go around and drag our criminal type guest around to the car. With a great deal of effort, I throw his body into the trunk and close it. I start to climb into the driver's seat then it dawns on me that if I grab the radio the hood had I may be able to tell if we have been observed.

After grabbing the radio I return to the car, jump into the driver's seat and drop the shift lever into reverse. As soon as I am in a position to do so, I put it into drive and head down the lane to the main road.

Chapter 9

We Make Good Our Escape

"Well it looks like you finally got something right Old Man," the kid says with a grin on her face.

This is the first time I have seen such an expression on her face since we met. "That may be Kid."

About the time we are patting ourselves on our backs the radio crackles into life.

"Hey Joel, Benny is gone and so is that guy's car. I think they got away. What do you want me to do anyhow?"

"Do you see them anywhere," is the return message from Joel"

"Naw, they are clean out of sight Joel. Do you want me to get to the car and see if I can catch them?"

Joel must be a little brighter than the rest of the bunch. His answer is, "No. Just get to our car and get out of here. I'll be doing the same thing as soon as I can get everybody gathered up. If those two are very far away you can bet it won't be very long until this hill is crawling with cops."

"Okay Joel. I'm on my way. Are you going to pick up the bodies?

"No way, we'll just leave them. The important thing right now is to get clear of this area, so get going."

I look over to see if Ginger has picked up on the word "bodies." If she has I am sure she's figured out that the odds are pretty good her mother is one of the bodies. She no longer has a smile on her face, but I don't see any grief there either.

About this time we come to the entrance ramp for the Interstate. I pull on it and head straight for Glen Falls. We make the twenty some miles in a little over fifteen minutes. As soon as we leave the Interstate I head straight to the sheriff's office. I hope Sheriff Hadley is on duty. I'm not too sure even a friend like him will believe a wild story like I am about to tell. He may think I have started trying to live the stories I write.

I park directly in front of the Sheriff's office, not wishing to walk any further than necessary before we are in the relative safety of the his office. As I step out of the car I hear a thumping noise coming from the trunk. I look over at Ginger, who has heard it also, and smile. "I guess our criminal has regained consciousness, but he can wait until after we talk to the Sheriff," I say while making my way to the door.

Upon my entering the door, Sheriff Hadley looks up from the file he is perusing and says, "Hey Ja, what brings you to my office? Are you in need of more police type stuff for your books or did you stop by to take me to dinner? Who is your little friend there?"

"Chuck I have a story to tell you that will outstrip anything I have ever written and probably most anything you have seen as Sheriff."

"Well, go ahead and spit it out then. You have my curiosity up and you know I am not a patient man."

"First, I think you need to come out to my car and take charge of the fellow locked in its trunk."

The Sheriff stands up so fast he almost knocks his chair over. What fellow," he asks while following Ginger and I out the door. I say again, using a sinister tone in my voice, "The one you hear pounding on my trunk lid, that's the fellow I am talking about Sheriff," I say while getting ready to open the trunk. "Maybe you had better be ready to subdue him Sheriff. However, I don't think he is in any shape to put up too much of a fight. He only has one arm that still works and he sort of has a dent in his head."

"Go ahead and open the trunk. I am ready for action if any is needed. I just can't wait to hear your explanation for this one."

I flip the remote and the trunk flies up. The crook doesn't even sit up. He just lies there bleeding from the head and moaning.

"Good Grief Ja, what did you do this guy? He's bloody and looks like he is about done in."

"First, I shot him with and arrow and then, three days later, I hit him over the head with a rock. I suspect that has something to do with his appearance Sheriff."

"Well I sure hope I never get on your bad side if this is the way you treat your enemies. I'll have my deputy take this guy over to the hospital and get him checked out while you tell me the rest of the story. I'm kind of anxious to hear this one. Maybe I'll be the one to write a book after we talk this time."

"Before I tell you the rest of the story Sheriff, maybe you had better send one of your deputies over to my place. If I am not mistaken there are at least four more of these fellows over there. We found Tom Hanson's body up the trail a few hundred yards from my cabin. He had been shot. I suspect one of this fellow's companions most likely killed him."

When we get inside the office, Sheriff Hadley tells his dispatcher to send a couple of cars up to my place and to radio the highway patrol. "Have them send some cars up as well. Tell them there may be some shooting so to be prepared," he adds as an after-thought.

Now the Sherriff turns to me and says "How did all this come about anyway? I never knew you to have any enemies Ja."

"Well Sheriff, meet Ginger. She's the cause of my involvement in this mess. I don't know a whole lot about what is going on either. All I know is I spotted Ginger out in the rain in front of my cabin. She was about to succumb to exposure. When I finally got her to come into my cabin she explained that a couple of men are chasing her and her mother. When the men were about to catch up with them Ginger's mother told Ginger to hide while she continued on up the trail. After the men passed Ginger, she started up the trail that led her to my cabin. The next morning the fellow that was in my trunk showed up. I shot him with an arrow before he could shoot us with his pistol. Oh, by the way, here is his pistol and spare clips. Ginger thinks these men are the ones that murdered her father a while back.

I turn and start toward the door and Ginger follows me. Before we make more than a few steps Sheriff Hadley says with a tone of excitement in his voice, "Just where do the two of you think you are going?"

"Right now my plan is to go by a store and pick up some clothes for Ginger and myself, then to get us adjoining rooms at the motel. Now that you have called in the cavalry we should be out of danger.

"Ja, you know I can't allow you to take the girl with you. You have no custody rights. I'll have to get the Division of Child Welfare over here to take care of her."

"Listen Chuck, the kid and I haven't had a bath in three days. In case you haven't noticed we don't smell too sweet. We haven't had a decent night's sleep for three nights. We have been living mostly on beef jerky for the past three days. We're tired, dirty and hungry. We just want to take care of these problems. After all, we been through a lot for three days now and haven't killed each other yet so don't you think you could wait until tomorrow morning to call in the authorities."

"Okay Ja, I'll do that. Their office is closed for the day so it would take quite a while to contact someone and get them over here anyway. You just make sure you have the girl back to my office by no later than nine o'clock in the morning. Okay?"

"Okay Chuck, we'll be here"

The thought of a shower and clean clothes is a driving force. I am so tired that I hardly remember stopping at the local department store and buying clothes. Ginger went into the preteen area and did her own shopping. I did my shopping and then waited for her to meet me at the checkout.
We stop at Mommy's Café and have a burger. The rest of the night is kind of a blur too. I rent adjoining rooms and the kid goes to sleep in her room and me in mine. When I wake up the kid is in bed with me.

It is about ten o'clock when we pull up in front of the Sheriff's office. Chuck is standing out front when we pull up. He meets me at the car before I can even get out. "Where have you been? That lady from Family and Children's Service has been about to eat me alive. She didn't appreciate me allowing you to keep Ginger over night. She's been lecturing me since nine o'clock about all the things that could possibly be going on."

"I'm sorry you got lectured Chuck, but I think the kid was better off staying with me than with some strangers last night."

"I do too so let's get inside and maybe we can present a unified front to the lady."

As soon as we step through the door Chuck introduces us to the lady from Family and Children's Service (FCS). Her name is Ms. Lipski. She never acknowledges the introduction she just says, "I want to talk with Ginger alone." As she is saying this she grabs Ginger by the arm and almost drags her into one of the interrogation rooms. The look on Ginger's face is one of pure terror.

I look over at Chuck to see if I can read anything in his face. It scares me that I can and what I read is not good. Chuck speaks before I even have time to ask any of the many questions on my mind.

"They found Tom Hanson's body and a female body. By the identification on her we are reasonable sure it is Ginger's mother," Chuck says with a bothered look on his face.

"How sure are you Chuck," I ask, almost afraid to hear the answer?

"Well, at this time we don't have a positive identification on her, but from what we found on her and in the car at the rest stop we are pretty sure. Do you know anything about any living relatives the girl has," Chuck asks while picking up his scratch pad to write down anything I might tell him.

"She mentioned grandparents, but I have no idea how to reach them. I had the feeling they were maternal grandparents so I don't think her last name will help you much in trying to find them." Then I go on to ask the question burning in my mind. "Did you catch any of the guys that were after us or did they get away?"

"We picked up four men when we made our raid yesterday. Two of them are local thugs and two of them are local tourist guides that sometimes work as trackers. I don't think they knew anything about what was going on. They thought they were on a rescue mission to rescue the girl. The State Patrol is questioning them now. The two guides are being very co-operative. The two thugs will only say they want a lawyer. It doesn't appear that there is any involvement of others, but we can't understand why the locals would have been involved with the people in suits you told me about. It just doesn't fit with the story you told me yesterday Ja. Anyway the State Patrol will want to talk to you and the girl later so you need to keep yourself available for a while."

About this time the door to the interrogation room opened. Ms. Lipski comes out still almost dragging Ginger with her. I look over at Ginger and for the first time since I met her she looks almost broken. As aggravating as she can be at times this look almost breaks my heart. I look the kid straight in the eye and say, "Come here kid, you look like you need a hug and I just happen to have one to spare." Before I finish saying the last word she runs to me jumps up throwing her arms around my neck and her legs around my waist. Her head is resting on my shoulder and she sobs so that her entire small body shakes like a leaf during a hurricane.

Ms Lipski is on her cell phone talking to someone. Chuck has this dumbstruck look on his face. I don't think he has ever seen my softer side before. Mostly this is because I have never had anyone to cause me to show it since he and I met. Anger wells up in me until it is about to spew out the top of my head like a geyser. Ms. Lipski must have told Ginger that her mother is dead. Why else would she be so upset. As soon as she gets off of the phone I walk over to her still holding the sobbing Ginger and ask, in not so polite a manner, "Did you tell Ginger that her Mother is dead?"

Ms. Lipski looks me straight in the eye and says, "No, she told me. She heard the shots when the men caught up with her mother. She knew they wouldn't leave her alive."

"You mean she knew her mother was dead the whole time she was with me?", I ask in almost total disbelief.

"Well, not exactly. She hadn't seen her mother dead, but as she said she knew they wouldn't have left her mother alive."

"Just what is the kid so upset about if she knew about her mother all along?"

"She wants to live with you and I told her she can't, at least not for now. I told her that we would have to do a complete background check on you before we would agree to allow you to be a foster parent. She told me about her grandparents and that they wouldn't want to take her. I talked to them and found out that she is at least partly right. They would be willing to take her except that the grandfather is terminally ill with lung cancer and the grandmother is wheelchair bound with arthritis. She said there are no other relatives on the maternal side, at least not in the United States. She and her husband escaped from East Germany in the seventies. They have lost track of their relatives in Europe. She said that Ginger's father claimed that he had no living relatives. She added that they never knew him well enough to know for sure."

"So you told Ginger that she couldn't go live with the only one in this world that she feels safe with and that she has to go live with total strangers. No wonder she is so upset." My temper is about to go off and I know that will not enhance the chance that Ms Lipski will allow Ginger to go with me. I try, very hard, to control my voice so my anger will not show though. I start out by saying, "If you do a case study on me I can assure you that you will find that my past is less than what would be desired in a foster parent. My present lifestyle is not what is needed for her benefit. I have little experience with the raising of young women because I was an alcoholic when my own daughters were Ginger's age and I didn't even live with them at that time, but as near as I can tell I am the only one Ginger feels comfortable with right now."

I fear that by the time I finish my speech I am no longer covering up my emotions with the tone of my voice. In fact, by the time I finish speaking, I am nearly yelling in the lady's face. Chuck's face is also turning red. I had no more than stopped yelling in Ms. Lipski's face than Chuck starts yelling at her.

"Ms. Lipski," he says, speaking slowly so as to make each word carries the meaning he would have it convey. He continued by saying. "I have known Ja since he came to this area. I make it my business to checkout strangers who move into my jurisdiction. I found him to be a recovering alcoholic, who sometimes had a problem keeping his hands from uncontrollably trembling. He was haunted by memories of things he could not forget and found he could not live with. He was trying to overcome these demons and it was none too clear that he would win his battle with them. But he did. He has become a good citizen, a good neighbor and good friend of mine. So I am going to vouch for him."

By the time Chuck is finished talking his voice is revealing his feelings very well. Ms. Lipski has a look on her face like she has only just survived a blitzkrieg.

When she regains her composure she says, "Ginger said she interviewed you. Is that right Mr. Davidson?"

I immediately protested, "She said she what? She interviewed me? She never interv—." My voice breaks in mid-word as I suddenly realize what all of Ginger's questions had been about. She knew her mother was dead or at least she was relatively sure of it. She knew that her grandparents were not about to take her in. She was interviewing me as a prospective replacement for her parents. Almost unable to speak I gasp out, "So that is what she was doing asking all of those questions. She was interviewing me."

"Yes Mr. Davidson, she told me that you are a good man that had spent the last four days protecting her. She said you are a Christian and that even though she is not, she thinks that Christians make the best parents. She said you are a brave man with a great deal of intelligence. She told me that you were the only one who ever took time to help her with her problems who wasn't being paid by her parents to do so. She said they never took the time to do so themselves. I have just come to the conclusion that you, Sheriff Hadley and Ginger have given me enough information that I can fill out most of the application form for prospective foster parents. I will have to make a home survey to be sure just what kind of environment I am putting Ginger into."

By now Ginger is no longer sobbing. She is just squeezing my neck but her head is still lying on my shoulder. As for me I am so flabbergasted that I can hardly speak. Finally I manage to squeeze out the words, "Sure, anytime you want to come by you will be welcome."

Ms Lipski says, "Would right now be a good time, Mr. Davidson?"

"Sure it would if Chuck is finished interviewing us."

Ms. Lipski looks over at Chuck and says, "Are you finished interviewing them Sheriff Hadley?"

"Yes, for right now, I am." Then Chuck looks over to me and says, "I'll drop by your place in a day or two. I'll need to go over a few things with you. Okay?"

"Okay Chuck. We plan to be there."

I look over to Ms. Lipski and say, "You had better follow me up to my cabin. It is rather difficult to find if you are not familiar with the area." Ms Lipski nods in agreement. With this we start toward the door of the sheriff's office.

Chapter 10

I Am to Become a Father Again

Ms Lipski follows us out of town and up Interstate 87. I can only imagine what is going through her mind as I take her further and further from civilization. When we finally turn up the lane to my garage, I suspect she is wondering what kind of recluse she is trusting Ginger's wellbeing to.

I park the car in front of my garage and Ms. Lipski parks directly behind me. When I step out of the car I half expect her to express her disapproval of my life style, but instead she just steps out of her car and motions for us to led the way. All the time we are walking up the path toward the cabin I keep thinking how appalling my lifestyle must seem to a modern lady of the world like Ms. Lipski.

When we reach the cabin door, I unlock it and motion for Ms. Lipski to enter. I start opening the shutters to allow light inside. When I enter Ms. Lipski is standing near the table where my laptop is sitting. I half expect her to say she has made a mistake trusting Ginger to my care and that they will be going now. Instead she opens her briefcase and pulls out what appears to be a form. She sits down at the table and motions that I should do the same. She looks up at me and then speaks "Your full name is?"

"John Edward Davidson," I respond.

"Permanent address?"

"Post office box 1277 Pottersville, New York."

"Occupation?"

"I am an author."

"What kind of author?"

"An author of books"

"What kind of books?"

"Books that sell, hopefully."

She continues asking the questions on the form and I continue answering them for what seems to be hours. When she reaches the bottom of the form she looks up and looks me straight in the eye and asks the question I was not expecting.

"Why do you want custody of this child?"

I had not given much consideration to this question. It just seemed the natural thing to do, but I am sure this would not be a very good answer to her question. After a few seconds of awkward silence I finally find my tongue and speak.

"I think I want the same thing for Ginger that you do. I want her to be where she will be protected, happy, well cared for, and loved. To be in an environment where she can flourish and grow up to be the lady that we both know she can be." If that means that I must give up custody of her then so be it."

"What kind of family do you think that would be John?"

"Thank you for calling me John. I wonder if I may call you by your first name and, if so, what is it?"

"You may call me Mary. Now please answer the question," she says with little emotion in her voice.

"I guess it would be a family like I grew up in. A two-parent, Christian family where the parents love each other and their children."

Again, she comes back with a question that I am at a loss for words to answer.

"Then what you are saying is you don't think you would be the best one to have permanent custody of Ginger?"

"Most likely not, Mary. I am nearly 60 years old. I am single. I am a recovering alcoholic. I am set in my ways. I have chosen to live a very isolated life; I have already had a family and horribly failed them. All and all I don't think this makes me very qualified to be Ginger's guardian, but if caring counts then take that into consideration, please."

"Caring does count John and you have already demonstrated that you care. You spent four very difficult and dangerous days protecting Ginger and I will see that is taken into account when I present your case. You will most likely be called in for a custody hearing if you are willing to do so. Now let's take a look to see what kind of a home you can offer Ginger."

I showed Mary around the cabin. I explain to her that Ginger will sleep in the loft. I show her the bathroom door and promise to hang it tomorrow. After showing Mary around my cabin and explaining its many strange features to her, Mary seems to be satisfied that it will do as a temporary residence.

She says, "I only have a few more questions for you John. What are you planning to do about school for Ginger?"

"I plan to see about getting her enrolled in the public school in Glen Falls tomorrow. If I were to become Ginger's guardian I would try to find a place to live in a town where Ginger could go to a public school. I think this is necessary for her social education. We will only use the cabin for weekends and summers."

Mary appears to be happy with my answer and turns to speak to Ginger, who had been listening to her fate being discussed. To my surprise she has been listening without saying anything. This is not like the Ginger I know.

"I will return the day after tomorrow to see how well things are working out for you and John. Goodbye Ginger. Goodbye John."

With these parting words Mary goes out the door and down the path. Ginger and I watch until she is out of sight. Then Ginger turns back into "The Kid".

"You aren't going to let that old biddy run our lives are you Old Man? I kept expecting you to stand up to her and tell her how things are going to be. How come you didn't do that anyway Old Man?" she says again putting great emphasis on the Old Man part.

"Listen to me Kid. Our society has laws. Some of them may not make a lot of sense at times, but they are what have been decided to be best for most people in our society. These laws say that it is the responsibility of the parents to raise their children. When parents are not an option then there are agencies set up to decide who would be best to take on the responsibility of raising the child. Even if their ruling goes against my interests I wouldn't want to change the system. I know it is not perfect, but it is the best we have and I intend to do what they say. I will never desert you Kid. You are in my life to stay. So let's just try to work together to make the best of it. Okay?"

I have tried to speak with compassion in my voice yet sounding firm in my convictions. I hope this has come through to the Kid. She needs to develop social skills. It appears that she has been raised in a vacuum, separated from her peers. I fear the Kid and I both have a great deal to learn about dealing with society.

CHAPTER 11

WE WALK AND TALK

I turn and start walking toward the door. When Ginger sees what I am doing she engages her mouth and spews out, "Where do you think you're going anyway Old Man?"

"I'm going after the backpack we left in the woods yesterday. Would you like to come along?"

"Sure, there's nothing to do around here anyway. Why do you want to live out here where there is nothing to do?"

"That's just exactly why I moved here Kid. It got me far away from the things I used to do."

"What things, Old Man? Like maybe drinking?"

"That would be one of them."

With this I turn and start walking toward the door. Ginger follows me. As we continue across the porch, down the steps and toward the garage Ginger doesn't say a thing. This makes me wonder what is going on in her little mind now. Other than for that few minutes this morning when she sobbed on my shoulder she has shown little emotion. That just isn't normal for a kid who has lost both her father and mother in a short period of time. This is to say nothing about her finding herself very much in harms way. I am determined to get into this kid's mind to see just what makes her tick.

"Well if you are going to stay here with me we will have to make arrangements for your education. What school did you attend, before all of this happened"

"I didn't go to any school Old Man," She says with a note of pride in her voice.

"You didn't go to any school! How were you getting your education then?"

"I was being home schooled," She says. Again there is a note of pride in her voice.

"By your mother?"

"No. I had a teacher who came to my home and taught me there."

"Well we will need to get in touch with her to find out your level of proficiency. Do you know how to get in touch with her?"

"No I don't. Mother sent her away before we left. I heard Mom tell her that she should go somewhere far away and leave no forwarding address because if the men watching us did not get the information, they were looking for from us, they might come after her. I assume she did what Mom suggested. She is a smart lady so I think she knew the gravity of the situation and took Mom's advice."

"There you go again Kid. You talk like a College student. You couldn't be any more than what, a fourth grader?"

"For your information Old Man, I was studying from sophomore and junior text books. I am smarter than most kids," she spews out like I must be dumb not to realize her level of intelligence.

"I've noticed your advanced level of education Kid. I have also noticed your near total lack of social skills. That's why we are going to enroll you in a public school," I say trying to speak with a sound of authority in my voice.

"You're going to do what? There's no way I'm going to a public school Old Man. You're a teacher. You told me so yourself. Why can't you teach me?"

"It's simple Kid. You can't learn to deal with society when you aren't exposed to it. What you have just told me explains several things about you that I have not been able to understand before. You will go to public school and that is that."

Ginger says nothing more after my speaking to her with a tone in my voice of one in authority. We have by now reached the garage. I stand at the back of the garage trying to get my bearings. Ginger walks up and puts her small hand in my hand. Maybe I am just being suspicious, but I have the feeling this kid uses her emotions to get her own way. Like the tears this morning. Did she shed those as a means of convincing Ms Lipski that she needed to be with me? Was that a show of bonding given only to gain her desires? I may be wrong, but I am going to watch very closely just to be sure I am not being conned by this adult-thinking kid. If what she is doing is a con job then she is good. In fact she is very good at using her emotions to manipulate situations in her favor. I hold Ginger's hand as if the emotions that caused her to put it there are genuine, but I am going to keep a watch out for a manipulative action that might follow this show of affection.

By now we have reached the location where I abandoned the backpack yesterday. I reach down, pick it up and start back down the trail. Ginger finally finds her tongue again and says, "You were just kidding about me going to a regular school weren't you. It would be so inconvenient. We would have to get up in the middle of the night to get me there on time. Don't you think it would be better for you to just teach me here, at the cabin? You're a schoolteacher. You could handle that couldn't you?"

"Sure I suppose I could brush up my skills and teach again but that isn't the point."

"What is the point then, Old Man?"

"There are a lot of lessons to learn in life and not all of them can be learned from books. It appears to me that you have a very good education from books, but you are lacking in some of the most basic life skills. This is the reason you need to go to public school. You need to be with your peers. You need to learn to function in normal life situations. That's why you are going to a regular school."

Seeing that this approach is getting her nowhere Ginger falls silent again. Upon reaching the garage I open the door and get the other backpack from the backseat of my car. We then walk in silence back to the cabin.

I set the backpacks in the kitchen and start going out the back door.

"Where are you going now, Old Man?"

"I am going to crank up the generator so I can use my power tools. I have to install the door on the bathroom remember."

"And just what am I supposed to do while you are doing that?"

"I don't know. There's a tablet and some pencils in the cabinet under my computer. Why don't you get them and maybe write or draw something. That will help keep your mind sharp. You will need to have a sharp mind when you go back to school."

Greatly to my surprise she does as I suggest. I continue with my project. In just a little over an hour my project is complete. Ginger has stayed busy writing on the tablet all the while. As I walk past her going to the kitchen I notice that she has written all numbers on the tablet. They are in groups and spaced almost like they are words. My curiosity gets the better of me.

"What is all of this anyway," I ask pointing to the numbers she has written.

"These are numbers my Father insisted that I memorize."

"What do they represent? They look almost like the code puzzles I work in my spare time."

Looking up from her work she says, "I have no idea what they represent. All I know is my father told my teacher that I was to memorize these numbers in the order I have them written down."

"What did your teacher have to say about your learning these numbers? Was she in favor of your doing so?"

"She said that as long as it didn't get in the way of my other studies it was fine with her. She said that she thought he just wanted me to develop a head for figures like his."

"Did your father take an active interest in your education?"

"As far as I know this is the only time he ever said anything about my education. My father wasn't one that you asked many question of. He did the telling and you did the listening."

All this made me very curious, but right now I am more hungry than curious so I just say, "Come on in the kitchen and help me fix supper Kid."

"I can't help you fix supper. Anyway it's dinner not supper."

"Call it whatever you want, but if you want to eat you had better help with fixing it."

"I'll help if you'll tell me what to do."

"That sounds like a deal to me. There are plates in the corner cabinet and the silverware is in this drawer. So you set the table and I will fix us some meat and potatoes."

After supper I clean up the mess myself. Ginger looks rather tired so I don't ask her to help, but she has a lot to learn about life's routine, daily chores. When I come out of the kitchen Ginger is sitting in my reading chair sound asleep. I just pick her up and carry her over and deposit her in the upper bunk. She doesn't wake up.

I sit down at my computer and start pushing the keys trying to catch up some on my writing. I have fallen so far behind my schedule that it will take a lot of key pushing in a short time to catch up. The problem is I, too, am sleepy. After about an hour of productive writing I am drained. I can't even write anything that interests me so I am sure I am not writing anything that will interest anyone else.

I have been so excited about this book up 'til now. I don't want to write if I am not writing at my best.

I blow out the lantern and get ready to crawl into bed.

CHAPTER 12

REVELATIONS

I wake up in a sweat about three-thirty in the morning. I've had another one of those dreams that sends chills up my spine like I have been hit with a few thousand volts of electricity. There is no use in trying to go back to sleep when I am so wired.

I quietly get out of bed and walk over to my computer table. I light the lantern, but keep it turned down as low as I can and still keep it lit. I guess I may as well try to write some more. When I reach over to turn on my computer I notice the paper that Ginger wrote the numbers on yesterday. I pick it up and look at the numbers for a few seconds. They look like the word puzzles in puzzle books. I work these sometimes when my mind just won't release the story I know is inside it.

I find myself picking up a pencil and starting to see if these numbers will cipher out to have any meaning. After a half hour or so I have come up with enough letters that I am fully convinced this is a message of some kind.

After working for another couple hours or maybe a little more, I have deciphered the coded message and it sends as much of a chill down my spine as my dream had. It is plain from this message that we are still in trouble, big trouble. Bigger trouble than I ever thought we were in. This is an entanglement bigger than any I have ever dreamed-up even for a plot in my books. I find myself sweating profusely even though it is rather chilly in the cabin.

I walk over to the bunks and shake Ginger's little arm to awaken her.

She just groans a little and then says, "What is going on Old Man? Why are you waking me up? It's still dark outside."

"I know Kid, but we have big troubles and it is time we get ready to get out of here. We need to do it fast, too. You get up and get dressed. Put on jeans, a flannel shirt and hiking boots. I will get the backpacks filled and the sleeping bags ready while you are doing that."

"What makes you think we are in so much trouble anyway?"

"I deciphered the numbers your father had you memorize. Believe me the message is scary"

"What is the message?"

"I'll give you all the details later, but right now we have more important things to do."

I don't know why it is, but every time I get in a hurry it seems the clock runs faster than normal. By the time I have our backpacks filled and the sleeping bags strapped on them it is full daylight. Ginger is ready too.

"Hey Kid, take a look out the front door. See if anyone is out there."

Ginger walks over and opens the door just a crack. She looks outside for a moment and then glances back at me and stammers, "Someone is out there and they are coming this way."

Instinct tells me to grab things and run, but common sense tells me I had better check out this intruder just to see how much danger we are in because of their being nearby. I grab my bow and quiver of arrows and move over to the door to check this out for myself. Before I reach the door Ginger says, "Look, its Ms Lipski"

I look through the crack in the door and observe that Ginger is right. It is Ms Lipski. What is hard to believe is the way she is dressed. She is wearing jeans, hiking boots and a tan leather jacket. I open the door and motion for her to come on in. When she reaches the porch steps she says, "You must have quite a hunting party scheduled. There are at least six guys down by your garage and a car followed me in with a couple more fellows in it."

"Did you notice anything different about these guys?"

"No John, they just looked like a hunting party to me."

After a few moments of hesitation she gets a frown on her face and says, "You know there was something rather curious about the guys in the car that followed me in. They were dressed in business attire and were wearing street shoes. I found out yesterday that is not a good way to dress when visiting you."

I start grabbing the backpacks with the bed rolls tie to them. I then quickly fold up the paper which the coded message is on, and cram it in my pocket. I grab Mary's arm and say, "come on we need to get a move on and we need to do it now."

Mary yanks her arm from my grasp and says, "What's going on here? Why do we need to get a move on anyway?"

"Mary, if my calculations are right I figure we have about five minutes left before we die or maybe worse. Is that reason enough to get a move on?"

"That's good enough reason for me John, but I will want an explanation when we have time for one."

I grab the other items I had laid out to take with us including the little black bag I always keep by the back door. I head out the door with Ginger and Mary close on my heels.

Mary gives me a strange look and says, "Aren't you going to lock your cabin before you leave it?"

"These guys are going to check it out, of this I am reasonable sure, so I am going to leave it open. That way they can get in without having to damage anything."

I hand Mary the second pack and shoulder the one I still have in my hand. We will be able to move much faster this time since Ginger need not carry a pack and I need not carry both packs. We head out the back door of the cabin and start walking up the nearest animal trail going uphill. After about twenty minutes of walking as fast as I can I stop and turn to see how far Ginger and Mary are lagging behind. When I do I almost get knocked down by Mary, who is right on my heels. Ginger is not far behind her. I guess I must have a surprised look on my face.

Mary with a grin on her face says, "I do a lot of hiking so this is not a new experience for me. Don't worry about me. I shouldn't need a rest until you do and Ginger is doing fine."

So far I neither see nor hear any signs that we are being followed. This is most likely a good time to exercise a covert maneuver of some kind to throw anyone following us off of our trail. The only problem is right now I just don't seem to have any such maneuver in mind. Since I have no better answer to our problem, I just keep walking up the trail. After only a few minutes another trail crosses the one we are on. It runs along the side of the mountain rather than up the mountain like the one we are on. I feel a tug on my sleeve and turn to see that it is Mary trying to gain my attention.

"I suggest that we might want to take this trail rather than to keep on going up hill. I am familiar with the area just a couple of miles to the north of here. I think, if we can get to that area, I can get us to a place where we can hide for a while and maybe make up some kind of a plan. I fear I cannot be of too much help unless I know a little more about what is going on here."

I say nothing I just turn on to the trail heading north and keep walking. I must admit it is much easier walking now that we are not walking uphill. I was about ready to take a rest when Mary suggests we take this trail. Now I feel that I can go on for some time before I need a rest. A quick glance over my shoulder is enough to tell me that neither Mary nor Ginger appear to be hurting. The further we get away from the cabin the better I will feel. Since it appears we got away without being observed by our pursuers they will have to resort to tracking us. This should be made more difficult by the fact that we, and a number of others, were all over this area earlier this week. Since there has been no rain or snow during this period it will be difficult, even for a good tracker, to tell which, is the freshest trail.,

While I have been lost in my own thoughts we have covered a good bit of distance. Again I feel a tug on my sleeve. I turn to face Mary.

"I suggest you let me take the lead for a while John. I recognize this area and I can lead us to a place that I think we can use for shelter as well as for concealment. Do you mind?"

"Not at all Mary, I welcome any help you can give. So you go ahead Ginger and I will follow your lead."

After about another half an hour Mary stops. She turns to me and says, "See that outcropping of rock up ahead. There is a small opening at the top of it, which leads down to a fair sized cave below. I don't think even most of the locals around here know about the existence of this cave. Do you want to risk going in?"

"I have no better plan Mary. My only concern is if we are found in there will we have a means of escape?"

"I think I have us covered on that count too, John."

"Okay then lets get inside and look this place over. If we have any doubts about staying I don't want to spend too much time here."

With that Mary again takes the lead. We walk up to the outcropping and climb up to the top. Mary is right. There is an opening. I pull the flashlight out of my pack and peer down into the hole. There is a rather steep decline down from the point of entry. I would guess a distance of about fifteen feet. I am not sure that we can climb back out of this hole if we go down.

"If we go down there can we get back out without a rope or something," I ask Mary?

"I've done it before John."

This is good enough for me. I remove my backpack and sleeping bag, since the hole is far too small for a man, to go though with anything on his back. I am not too sure we will be able to get the packs though, but we manage to do so after removing the sleeping bags. Mary goes down first since she is familiar with the cave. I lower Ginger down to Mary's waiting arms. Then I squeeze down through the hole myself. As I am going through the entrance I notice there is a fair amount of air being drawn downward through it. This is good news for several reasons. The cave is ventilated so we need not worry about a lack of oxygen for us to breathe or to have a fire. The smell of the smoke will not drift back to the trail if the trackers track us this far. Lastly there has to be another entrance somewhere or there would be no airflow. All-in-all, this is good.

Once we are inside we realize the cave is totally dark except right under the entrance. I rue the fact that I put the flashlight back in the pack before dropping it down into the cave. After repositioning the pack to the small shaft of light I manage to find the flashlight. I hand it to Mary and explain, "This is just a two cell flashlight and I only have two changes of batteries for it. We will need to use it sparingly.

It is not only dark in the cave, it is cold and a damp as well. I tell Mary, "I will go get some dry wood so we can build a fire. Why don't you and Ginger find a place for us to spread out our sleeping bags?" With that said I walk over and start climbing out the entrance hole. I make it back outside without too much of a problem if I neglect to mention the skin lost on my elbows and knees.

I stay on the uphill side of the rock outcropping so as to not disturb nature enough that it will be easily observed from the trail below. There is plenty of dry wood around, but I fear it is not exactly campfire size. This will require me to do a lot of chopping with that little hand axe I brought along.

After about an hour of pulling, dragging and tugging I finally have enough wood at the entrance to last us for quite some time. I call down into the cave entrance for Mary to bring me the hatchet. When I get the hatchet I start cutting the limbs into pieces that are small enough to get through the entrance. I will cut them down to a more usable size after I have them in the cave. I am careful to keep chips of wood from flying back down toward the trail. We don't need anything like these wood chips showing near the trail that appears to be freshly made.

Before I climb back down into the cave I have Mary go to the area she has selected for our campsite and shine the flashlight in every direction while I look down through the cave entrance. I can see nothing. Finally satisfied that all we need to do outside the cave, at least for now, is complete. I again squeeze myself through the tiny entrance.

CHAPTER 13

FINALLY AN OPPORTUNITY TO COMPARE NOTES

Once inside Mary and I gather up all the wood we can carry while Ginger holds the flashlight for us. Once we each have our arms full of wood Ginger leads us back to the area she and Mary selected for our campsite. I make some shavings and lay small sticks on top of them. In a few minutes we have a fire going. There is a stream flowing down through the lowest part of the cave, but it is well below our campsite. I inspect the walls to see if I can determine a waterline. That will give us an idea of how high the water may come up during a heavy flow. I find nothing that gives me much of an indication. Most likely a flood would only come in the springtime. I sure intend to be out of here well before then. Mary has spread out the sleeping bags and emptied the backpacks. I sit down on a rock a few feet back from the fire. Mary is the first to speak.

"Now that we are settled down and safe for the moment would you mind explaining to me just why we are here and what danger we are in?"

I reach in my pocket and hand Mary the piece of paper Ginger had written the numbers on with my deciphered letters above each number.

C	O	D	E	D		M	E	S	S	A	G	E		B	E	L	O	W
7	23	1	10	1		18	10	12	12	11	15	10		8	10	17	23	21

C	O	N	T	A	I	N	S		L	O	C	A	T	I	O	N
7	23	5	22	11	25	5	12		17	23	7	11	22	25	23	5

O	F		A		L	I	S	T		O	F		P	E	R	S	O	N	S
23	24		11		17	25	12	22		23	25		2	10	16	12	23	5	12

I	N		G	O	V	E	R	M	E	N	T		A	N	D		I	N
25	5		15	23	13	10	16	18	10	5	22		11	5	1		25	5

O	R	G	A	N	I	Z	A	T	I	O	N		W	I	T	H
23	16	15	11	5	25	3	11	22	25	23	5		21	25	22	20

E	V	I	D	E	N	C	E		K	E	Y		H	E	R	E
10	13	25	1	10	5	7	10		6	10	9		20	10	16	10

35	48	19	37	25	50		48	25	25		47	39	25		58	38	40	25	24

42	44	31	44	34	48	56	39	15		58	25	40	41	43	39	22	45

Mary looked at it for a moment then with a look of total dismay on her face she says, "What organization and what government officials?"

"Your idea is as good as mine Mary. All I know is somebody or some group was chasing Ginger when I found her. She said her mother was leading the men away from her. Later she told me her father had been killed a short time ago and there had been men watching her and her mother ever since. They were in the process of trying to escape these men when they started up the mountain from the rest stop. Ginger told me her mother said "her father had been killed by the men he was working for". Yesterday when I was installing the bathroom door Ginger got bored. I told her where she could find some paper and a pencil so she could entertain herself while I was working. Later I saw this paper lying where she left it. When I asked her what it was she told me it was a sequence of numbers her father had told her teacher to have her memorize. This morning when I woke up I became curious to see if they would decipher out to have any meaning. What you read is what I deciphered."

"What makes you so sure the men at your garage were the men referred to by Ginger's father?"

"I am not sure, but I wasn't willing to go ask them if they were there to shoot Ginger and I. Then when you said two of them were wearing suits I was sure they were not here to hunt game. In all the years I have lived up here I have only seen men up here in suits one other time. That was when the men who were trying to kill Ginger appeared. Now, what are you doing up here today? You said you wouldn't be back until tomorrow.'

"I know John, but when I got back to my office I learned the coroner had released Ginger's mother's body to her parents. They have arranged her funeral service and burial for tomorrow. So I had little choice but to come up and let you know."

"I am sure glad you didn't come dressed in your street clothes."

"I learned my lesson about that yesterday. Besides I told my supervisor since I was going to be up in this area I was going to take the rest of the day off and do some hiking."

"That's bad, but your husband will report you missing when you fail to come home tonight, won't he?"

"I have no husband John. My husband and both my sons were killed in an auto accident two years ago."

"Oh. I am sorry Mary. I didn't mean to bring up something so hurtful." Then after a few seconds hesitation, I continued, "Since you are not expected back until tomorrow no one will realize we are missing until we fail to show up at the service for Ginger's mother. That will give these guy's well over twenty-four hours to find us before the local authorities realize we are missing."

"What do you suggest we do next, John?"

"We need to get the information we have to the authorities, but it is just too risky to try getting out of here now. By tomorrow it will be known that we are missing so the police will start looking for us, which means the people tracking us will either have left or they will be the ones being tracked. I guess, for now, we should just sit tight. I'm going to try to decipher the rest of the numbers Ginger wrote down. What I have deciphered so far is a very simple code, but the remaining numbers are a different code and it appears to be a much more sophisticated code than I have deciphered thus far. It is almost likely Ginger's father wanted the first part of the message to be simple enough that most anyone could decipher it, but the second part he made difficult enough that it would require a cryptologist to decipher it."

All the while Mary and I have been talking she has been preparing a meal for us. She has selected some tined meat and fruit. She divided it into three separate portions and set a portion in front of each of us. As Ginger reaches for her portion I reach over and push her hand back.

"We need to say grace first Kid."

"Yeah Old Man, I forgot.

After saying grace we each eat in silence. Ginger finally breaks the silence by saying, "Hey Old Man, do you really believe in that God and Jesus thing?"

"Yea, Kid I really do believe."

Ginger hesitates for a moment or two then she says, "My Mom told me that all religions are just fairy tales that weak people rely on to give them strength. You seem strong enough why do you need to rely on religion."

"Kid, some of the strongest people I have known, people much stronger than me, rely on religion. I don't think they rely on it because they are weak, but because it makes sense. Man is the most superior life form on earth. Some are very intelligent. Some have great abilities. Some are great designers. Some are great engineers. Some are great builders, but none can create. They can only use the raw materials available to them. Raw materials which were created by someone else. That someone else must be a supreme being. And as for Jesus, it only makes sense to me that the Supreme Being who created all of this and gave it to man must love us very much. He must love us enough to be willing to send His own son to us, to teach us and to die for us so we can see just how strong His love for us is. All of creation is just too perfect to be nothing more than an accident, as nonbelievers tend to say. I can no more explain where God came from than the nonbelievers can explain where the raw materials came from, but believe me Kid, God exists just as sure as you and I do."

Ginger pipes up in her usual upsetting way of questioning my answer "What has Jesus ever done for you?"

"Everybody is always looking for what Jesus can do for them. Well, I have news for them Kid, Jesus has already done His part. We should be asking what we can do for Jesus. When we start to serve Jesus is when the real miracle of God's love starts to bless our lives. Not in a material way, but in spiritual way. Life begins to make sense and be satisfying when we do for others. That is the true miracle of God's love."

Ginger sits in silence for a minute or two then says, "Yeah, you may have a pretty good point there Old Man. I will want to talk to you some more about this when we are in a little safer place to do so."

Mary says nothing for a while, but I have observed a look on her face that indicates this is about to change.

Finally she says, "Honestly! I can't believe you two. You call each other Kid and Old Man and act like you have no respect for each other at all. I have just sat and listened to one of the most beautiful Father, Daughter talks I have ever been privileged to hear. It is obvious even for a casual observer that the two of you have strong feeling for each other yet you talk to each other like a couple of snarling cats. What is with all of this outward disrespect when there is such inner warmth? Can you explain this to me either of you? If so, please do."

"I don't know how to explain it Mary. I started call Ginger Kid when we first met and I didn't know her name. After we learned each other names I continued to call her Kid because of the lack of respect she showed. She started calling me Old Man as a way of getting even with me for calling her Kid. I have just kept calling her Kid because of her defiant attitude and she has kept calling me Old Man for revenge."

"Well, I suggest the two of you quit addressing each other as Kid and Old Man before you petition the court for final custody. Not everyone may see the genuine feeling you have for each other as I do. It could have a bearing on the outcome of the custody ruling."

"I'll keep that in mind Mary and thanks for caring enough to point it out to us."

I lean back against a large rock near the fire and start studying the coded message again. If only I had my computer maybe I could speed up the process of decoding the final portion of this message.

After only a short time I grow tired of studying the message without making any headway. Ginger has taken over the job of keeping the fire going. Mary has, by now, set up our campsite. Everyone is doing their own thing and no one has spoken for some time.

Finally I break the silence by asking Mary, "You said you are familiar with this cave. Is there another way out of it that is big enough for us to make it through?"

"I'm not sure. My youngest son found this cave while we were hiking up here. Bill, that was my husband, and I entered it. When we found it was easy enough to get in and out of we allowed our boys to join us inside and we did some exploring. We never found the other entrance, but we were sure it existed because of the ventilation."

"Maybe we should look for it now. It would be nice to know another way to get out of here if it became necessary."

"It shouldn't be too hard to find. All we have to do is to walk the direction the air is flowing." With this she picks up the flashlight and motions for me to follow her. Ginger agrees to stay behind to keep the fire going.

After walking for an indeterminate time with Mary in the lead she stops and turns the flashlight out. I hadn't noticed it before Mary turned the flashlight off, but there is a faint bit of light here. We look in all directions, but cannot determine where it is coming from. Then Mary turns the flashlight on and points it straight up. We are standing under a shaft winding its way upward. When Mary turns the flashlight off again it is plain too see where the light is coming from. We also notice the air is flowing up the shaft. This must be the other outlet. Sometimes luck is bad and then again sometimes it is ridiculous. This is one of the ridiculous times. There is no way we can climb out of here through that small an opening. We very well may be trapped in here if the trackers find us.

I check my watch. It is four o'clock. It will be getting dark soon. I am not sure if the trackers will try tracking us after dark. I suspect they may be desperate enough to do just that. I can only hope they will stop since tracking is difficult enough during the day and it is near impossible at night.

I guess Mary has been lost in her own thoughts also since she, too, has said nothing. Finally, she breaks the silence by saying, "I guess we may as well go back. There is no way for us to get out of here through that small an opening." With this she turns and starts back the way we had come. Suddenly it dawns on me I have just followed Mary. I don't have the slightest idea how to get back to our campsite. Mary is walking at her normal stride so I just keep following her. I am surprised when the campfire appears dead ahead of us. Mary is pretty proficient in nature's outback.

CHAPTER 14

THE INADEQUACY OF WORD

When we reach our campsite we find Ginger sound asleep atop one of the sleeping bags. I reach down and pick up her limp, little body. Mary unzips the sleeping bag and I lay Ginger down. Mary zips the sleeping bag up again. Ginger never even flinches during the whole procedure.

Mary says, "Go ahead and take the other sleeping bag John. I'll sleep leaning against the rock close by the fire. I can sleep sitting up. It doesn't bother me."

"No Mary, you take the sleeping bag. I don't sleep too well most of the time anyway. Besides, now that we know there is no other way out of here I think I will spend most of the night watching the entrance. I sure don't relish getting caught in here. The way a bullet would ricochet off these cave walls each shot would have several opportunities to do one of us in."

"I don't think I will sleep very well either John. Why don't I make us some coffee and I will keep you company for a while. With this she picked up one of the canteens and poured water into two of the canteen cups. After setting both at the edge of the fire she lies back on one elbow, but says nothing for a long while.

I notice a look on her face that became very familiar to me in Nam. It is the look of having suddenly lost someone very close to you. I also know the feelings of this state. Confusion, questions of your own beliefs, the why them and not me. I finally break the silence, which is so thick it can be cut with a knife. "Are you all right Mary?"

Mary glances up and then says, "This is very hard for me. I haven't been able to hike, camp or even spend time in the woods since the death of my husband and boys. Everything here reminds me of them. I am sorry. I shouldn't be burdening you with my personal problems. It is not very polite of me to do so"

"Don't worry about being polite to me. I spent so much time on the street that I am very familiar with impoliteness. Besides I don't think having feelings you cannot hide is being impolite. Tell me about your family if it isn't too difficult for you to do so."

Mary starts by saying "My husband and I met in college. We were both studying archaeology. I kept seeing him in my classes. One day as I was leaving one of these classes he walked up beside me and just walked with me. He never said a word. Finally I asked him for a date. He accepted. That was the beginning of our lives together. After we graduated we went on a couple of digs together. It was fun, but we wanted a normal life together. Bill started writing articles for magazines, mostly articles about archaeology. I continued my education until I was qualified to become a professor of archaeology. A couple of years later I became pregnant. After James was born I became a stay-at-home mom. Then, just a little less than a year later, I became pregnant again. When William II was born our family was complete. Life was like a fairy tale. Oh, we had the normal problems. Mostly financial, but all-in-all we had a fine life together. When the boys were old enough to walk for some distance we started taking them on hikes and then later on camping trips. We all enjoyed digging for artifacts. These mountains are full of them, as I am sure you are aware. We were coming back from one of these outings when a drunk driver came across the centerline right into the path of our automobile. Bill and William were killed outright. James lived for a few days. Then the doctors told me he had no brain activity. He had been brain-dead since the crash. I had to give them permission to turn off his life support. I, for reasons I will never understand, was not even seriously hurt in the accident."

I look over and noticed that Mary is shaking. "Are you cold?"

"Yes, just a bit I guess."

"Why don't you crawl into the sleeping bag? I will finish making the coffee. Maybe being in the sleeping bag and a little hot coffee is just what you need."

Mary looked at me with tears welling in her eyes and says, "I can't. I just can't climb into that sleeping bag. I may never be able to sleep in one again as long as I live. There are just too many memories associated with this life style. I'm sorry to burden you with all of this, John. I haven't spoken of these things to anyone in the two years since their deaths. I don't know why I am telling you all of this now."

"Do you have nightmares Mary?"

"Yes, I do. I relive that crash most nights and, if it is not the crash, it is the doctor turning off my son's life support."

"I wish I knew words that would comfort you, but I fear that I have no words that will comfort a wound as deep as the one you bear. I have made an extensive study of words; first as a student, later as a teacher and now as an author but I fear I have found there are many occasions when words fall short of their speaker's intent. I fear this is one of those occasions."

While I have been talking, Mary has completed making our coffee. She hands me a cup, her hands still shaking. I take the coffee and then motion for Mary to come and sit next to me. To my surprise she moves over beside me. I put my arm around her shoulders and rub her arm trying to warm her enough that she will stop shaking. From the look she gives me I think this small gesture has conveyed my sympathy much better that the most eloquent words could have. We sit sipping our coffee each lost in our own thoughts. Finally Mary says, "Ginger tells me you would never tell your wife about your experiences in Vietnam. She said you told her you didn't want to cause your wife to have nightmares like yours. Well, I just want to let you know that if it would help, if it would help at all, you can tell me about them. You see I already have nightmares of my own. I might even welcome having some that were different than the ones I keep having over and over again."

Neither of us speaks again and after a short time I notice Mary has fallen fast asleep. I am reluctant to move my arm from around her for fear I might wake her from this peaceful sleep. I know how precious peaceful sleep is when you are plagued with post-trauma stress syndrome.

After a while it becomes necessary for me to move to put some more wood on the fire or it is going to go out. I gently slip my left arm under Mary's legs while keeping her head snuggled against my right shoulder and lift her. She doesn't even appear to be aware of my movement so I carry her over to the open sleeping bag and lay her on it. I pull the other side over her limp body and zip her in.

I spend the rest of the night keeping the fire going. Ever so often I find myself waking up after having dozed off for a bit. Each time I do I take the flashlight and move over to where I can see if anyone has found the cave and is coming our way. Each time I find no sign of light anywhere except for the flashlight I am carrying and the fire.

After my umpteenth trip I am finally able to see some light coming in from the cave opening. It must be daylight now. I walk back to our campsite and put a canteen cup filled with water on the fire to heat for coffee. When it has come to a boil I pour in the coffee grounds and stir it until it is about the color coffee should be. Mary's sleep has become restless so I would guess she is experiencing the nightmares she told me about.

I walk over and gently touch her shoulder to wake her up. She wakes with a jerk and sits up straight in the sleeping bag. "I am sorry I didn't mean to startle you, but it is daylight and I think we need to check on our situation soon. I have some coffee ready."

"I am glad you woke me John. I was having a nightmare. It is good to be awake. Did you stay awake all night?"

"I dozed off a few times."

"How did Ginger sleep?

“Ginger slept peacefully all night. I don’t think she had nightmares, but I think we should let her sleep for a while yet. I’ll make breakfast as soon as I finish my coffee.”

“Just what do we do now?”

“After breakfast we will break camp and head back to town. I don’t think these people are dumb enough to stay around after we are known to be missing. I expect to be able to walk out of here unmolested.”

“And if you are wrong. What then?”

I don’t know Mary. Let’s just pray that I am not wrong I guess.

Chapter 15

Sometimes the Truth is Difficult to Believe

We pack our backpacks and roll up our sleeping bags. Ginger, using the flashlight to find her way, leads us to the cave entrance.

Upon reaching the entrance I set down the pack and sleeping bag and started climbing out the entrance. Trying to squeeze my bulk out this hole is something akin to trying to put a tutu on an elephant. There just isn't much room to spare. After a few minutes of struggle I am out far enough to observe the surrounding area. All appears to be clear so I climb on out.

I turn and look down the hole. "Mary hand Ginger out to me."

Mary says nothing. She just passes Ginger up to my waiting hands. After I have Ginger out I turn to reach back down into the hole to help Mary out, but I find her already out and standing behind me.

I start down the hill to the trail with Mary and Ginger right on my heels. When we reach the trail I motion for them to stop. "I will take the lead for now. We need to stop every few yards to look and listen to see if anyone is nearby. The problem is we will have no idea if they are friends out looking for us, or foes out to do us in. I would rather avoid seeing anyone at all rather than try to figure out it they are friend or foe. This is especially true if they are foes because they might identify themselves by shooting at us. I have a very distinct dislike of being shot at."

We move down the trail until it merges with the one that leads back to my cabin. Still in the lead, I turn onto this trail and we continue to move along in our jerky fashion. We move this way until we are near enough to my cabin to see it. I then angle us off the trail and walk, through the woods just out of sight of the cabin, toward the garage and our cars. To my surprise we arrive at the garage without meeting anyone along the way. Mary's car is sitting in the drive directly behind the garage door. No one is in sight.

"Where are we going John, Mary asks as I am opening the garage door?

"I am heading straight for Sheriff Hadley's office. Maybe he can help us sort out some of this mess." While I am saying this I am also opening the trunk of my car and throwing in the backpacks and our other gear.

"I'll meet you there, John. I am going to stop by my office for a few minutes first."

With this last statement Mary gets in her car and drives off toward the highway. Ginger and I climb in the car and take off not far behind Mary. The trip into town is uneventful, greatly to my surprise. I half-expected someone to force us off of the road or take pot shots at us, but nothing happens, nothing at all. When we reach town I drive directly to the Sheriff's office. Sheriff Hadley is walking down the street toward his office. It appears that he is just returning from the café up the street.

When he sees me getting out of my car he hollers over to me. "Just where have you two been! I was just about to send half the law enforcement personnel in this area out looking for you. When you didn't show up for the funeral this morning we assumed the worst. By the way, you wouldn't have any idea where Ms Lipski might be, would you? She seems to be missing too"

"Yes, Mary was with us. She said she was going to stop by her office for a few minutes and then she would be coming over too."

"Oh, so it's Mary now is it?" Chuck says with a sound of surprise in his voice.

By this time we are in the Sheriff's office where Chuck motions for Ginger and I to be seated. Then he says, in a somewhat calmer voice than before, "Where have you been anyway?

"Okay Chuck I'll tell you the whole story. The day before yesterday I saw a set of numbers Ginger had written down on a paper. When I ask her what they were she said "They were a sequence of numbers that her Father had told her teacher to have her memorize". I didn't think too much of it at the time, but I couldn't help but notice how much they looked like the puzzles I work where numbers represent letters. I woke up early yesterday and, out of boredom, I picked up the paper Ginger had written the numbers on and I started working them like a number puzzle to see if I could make words out of them. Well, I did. Here I'll show you," I say while reaching into my pocket and pulling out the paper I have been carrying. "Take a look and see what you make of this, "I say while handing the paper to Chuck."

Chuck looks at the paper for a few seconds. The look on his face is the look of a kid who has just been handed a test paper and realizes he has no idea what the answers are to all of those many questions. He opens his mouth and points his index finger at me, but stops short of saying anything. Finally he says, "I suppose you know nothing else about this?"

"No, honestly I don't, Chuck,"

"Tell me, just how did Ms Lipski get involved in this with the two of you?"

"She came up to my cabin yesterday to let Ginger and I know that the funeral had been moved up to today. She showed up at my cabin shortly after I had deciphered the number code. I was in the process of packing up enough gear for Ginger and I to spend a few days in the woods if necessary. Ginger was checking the front of the cabin to see if anyone was watching us or coming after us when she says "Ms Lipski is coming up the trail". I told Mary that I thought we might be in danger. She said that there was a hunting party gathering near my garage. She said a car had followed her up the road to my garage. Then it dawned on her that the men in the car that followed her in were wearing business attire. That was good enough for me to decide that we should head for the hills. Mary went with us and even helped find a good hiding place."

When I finish talking I stand up and start toward the door with Ginger hot on my heels.

Chuck says, "And just where do you two think you are going anyway?"

"It's been a long time since breakfast and all of the hiking we did created a mighty hunger in me. When I started hearing Gingers tummy growling I thought it would be a good idea if we got ourselves something to eat so we are going down to Mommy's Café."

"Are you planning to go back to your cabin anytime soon?"

"No, I think we will stay in town until you can find out something about the meaning of the note I gave you. We will be staying at the motel if you need us for anything. Otherwise we will check in with you in the morning. Is that all right with you?

Chuck shakes his head with a look of disbelief on his face and then says, "Sometime I would like for you to explain to me just how I became your employee."

About this time Mary walks in the door. Chuck looks over at her and says, "If you are hungry you may as well go with them to get something to eat, but I will want to get a statement from you later."

Mary says nothing she just turns and walks out the door with Ginger and I. In fact nothing is said by any of us until we sit down at the table in Mommy's Café.

"Mary finally breaks the uneasy silence by saying, "What are you two going to do now? You aren't going back to the cabin are you?"

"No I'm going to get us adjoining rooms at the motel and then we are going shopping for some new clothes. I don't intend to go back to the cabin, at least not to stay, until we know a little more about what is going on. Chuck is doing some investigating to see if he can shed any light on our situation. Would you like to come shopping with us? I am sure Ginger would like to have a woman shopping with her much more than having me tag along behind her."

"Yes I would, but first I need to tell both of you something. I have been removed as the social worker in charge of your case. They say I have become too personally involved with the two of you." Seeing that Ginger and I both are opening our mouths to speak Mary goes on to say, "Now before either of you speak let me say that I agree with this decision. I am too close in my feeling to be as objective in the investigation and in making decisions as a social worker should be. Now let's go shopping.

Nothing more is said by any of us. I just pay the bill, leave the waitress a tip and we walk out and get in our cars. One thing about a small town you don't need to spend much time deciding where to shop. There is only one, really nice department store in town.

When we reach the parking lot Mary parks and I park next to her. Mary leads the way into the store and immediately goes to the women's and girl's clothing department. I tag along, but when she and Ginger start discussing what kind of bra Ginger needs I beat a hasty retreat for the men's department. I hadn't even noticed that Ginger needed one. After nearly an hour Mary and Ginger look me up so I can pay the bill. I bought myself a couple of changes of clothes and a new belt. Ginger has enough outfits to last her a couple of weeks. I never had that many clothes in my life. Oh Well, I guess girls need more clothes than we guys do. We don't usually care all that much about how we look.

With the shopping taken care of I thought it would be a good idea to get us rooms at the motel. I would hate to have them all taken before we secure a couple for ourselves. Mary leaves us and goes back to work.

After we secure adjoining rooms for ourselves we head back to Sheriff Hadley's office to see what he has learned about our pursuers. When we reach the Sheriff's office we find Chuck on the phone. I am not sure who he is talking to, but he doesn't sound any too happy with what he is hearing.

When Chuck hangs up I ask him, "Did you find out anything about the note?"

"I've been on the phone ever since you left. I've talked to the FBI, the State Patrol, most of the local sheriffs, and police departments in the surrounding area. The general consensus is that this is all the product of a very intelligent young mind with too much time on her hands. The FBI says they investigated Ginger's father's business in conjunction with the Interstate Commerce Commission when he was killed and found nothing out of the ordinary. None of the local departments know of anything going on out of the ordinary. I don't know what more I can do."

I look over at Ginger. She is so mad that she is almost red in color. I figure I better speak first so I ask Chuck, "Don't you believe us?"

"Sure I believe you Ja, but what do you want me to do. I am just a small time county sheriff. I can't be telling these huge agencies how to conduct their business. By now, half of them are upset with me for the amount of prying I have done and my insistence that they look further into this matter. They consider this a local matter and I don't expect too much more help from any of them. Oh, by the way, Ms. Blanchard from the child welfare office called she wants you and Ginger in her office now. From the way she sounded I think you had better be getting yourselves over there"

"Okay Chuck we are on our way. I would, however; be pleased if you would keep an ear out for any new information that might come your way about anything concerning Ginger or me."

"I'll do that Ja. Now you had better be getting yourself over to that social worker's office. She sounded pretty uptight."

We hardly have the CFS office door open when this middle-aged woman starts toward us with her mouth wagging and her finger waving. She escorts us into her office and motions for us to be seated.

"I'm Ms. Blanchard. I don't mind telling you that if I had been handling this case from the beginning you wouldn't have custody of this girl. I guess I am stuck with the court ruling but I am going to be keeping a close watch on both of you. I can't believe that anyone would even consider granting you custody of a little girl like this. You're an ex-alcoholic, an ex-street person, a father, who by his own admission, has failed to provide for the welfare of his own children and you are a near recluse living out in those woods."

I never knew anyone could talk that long without taking a breath. I think about listing all the things I have done trying to protect Ginger, but decide that she most likely would find fault with that as well. I just sit quietly and hold my breath that Ginger will stay quiet as well.

"After Ms. Blanchard catches her breath she asks, what are your plans for providing for the needs of this child?"

When Ms. Blanchard calls Ginger "this child", I can see the hair on Ginger neck bristle until it almost stands straight out. Somehow, though, she manages to keep enough control of herself that she doesn't speak.

"I have rented us adjoining rooms at the motel for tonight. This afternoon I intend to take Ginger and enroll her in school. Tomorrow, I will start looking for a place for us to live here in town during the school year. This is about as far as we have planned ahead. I'll keep you informed as to the progress of our plan and of any future plans we make."

"You had better do just exactly that if you want to retain custody of this child", Ms. Blanchard says with a snarl on her face that even a big cat would envy.

With that she dismisses us like we were a couple of school children. Ginger and I turn and walk out the door and to my car.

When we are in the car, Ginger starts letting out all the things that have been boiling up in her this afternoon. When she speaks the words explode form her mouth like they are being pushed out by a class four hurricane. "I suppose you don't believe me either. Where do all these people get off treating me like a mere child? Their not believing me is going to put me in a position to be killed. What are you going to do about that anyway Old Man?"

"Right now I am going to take you to the local junior high school and see if we can get you enrolled, Kid!"

"You know that if we stay where I can be found I'll be killed, don't you?" You aren't gong to let that happen are you?"

"No, I have no intention of allowing us to fall further into harms way. I don't intend to prove to these people that we are right about being in danger by one or both of us getting shot. However; for right now, we need to make the moves that convince Ms. Blanchard we are doing exactly what we told her we would be doing."

Chapter 16

We Try We Fail

It turns out getting Ginger enrolled in school is not as easy as I had thought it was going to be. First, we have nothing to show what her education level is. Second, we have nothing showing what her age is. Third, there is no way they believed Ginger when she tells them her level of education.

After checking with the state and getting Ginger's records they refuse to believe the information they receive. Her being without identification, they concluded that the information is not her information. Either she must be lying about her name or there is a mix-up at the state level. It is finally resolved by their setting a date for testing Ginger. After this is done they will determine Ginger's grade. These tests will need to be ordered from the state and will not be available for a couple of days.

By the time we finally conclude our business with the school officials it is almost time for dinner. I wish I had some way to get in touch with Mary. I sure could use a conversation with someone friendly right now. After dealing with law officials, Ms. Blanchard at the child welfare office and then the school officials it would be nice to be around someone who believes what Ginger and I have to say.

Ginger and I walk out of the school building, climb into my car and take off before either one of us speaks. I am not looking forward to what Ginger is likely to say after spending the entire afternoon being talked to like a child and talked about in ways that are very upsetting to her. However; when she does speak what she says surprises me more than what she might have said which would have upset me.

After riding in silence for some time she says, "John, I love you. You are the only one that has treated me like a person and not like a mere child. You've done more with me and for me than anyone in the world has ever done before, without being paid. I can't visualize my life without you in it. Please tell me you will keep me with you. I am begging you. I am so scared."

She stops talking with this last statement, but I know she has more she wants to say. Maybe she just can't find the words she wants to use or maybe it is just so hard for her to admit that she needs help since she is so independent. I am so taken aback by her expression of love for me that I have a hard time putting together the words I will use responding to her. Oh, what the heck. I'll just let my heart do the talking and not worry that my words are technically correct or that they are the best chosen words for the occasion.

"I love you too, Ginger and, as I have told you before, I am in your life for as long as we both live. Regardless of how all these problems facing us are resolved it will be you and me working together. As for you being frightened, I understand that as well. I am frightened too. It is frightening knowing that there are people dedicated to the idea of killing you. I only wish I could guarantee you that all will work out for the best but I can't do that. I will, however; guarantee you that I will do everything in my power to make things work out right for us."

By this time we are at the motel. I help Ginger get her new clothes out of the car and carry them into her room. In an effort to get Ginger's mind off of the weighty thoughts of our survival and of her future I suggest she try on her new clothes. I have noted, though I am no expert on the subject of women's moods, trying on new clothes seems to have a soothing effect upon them. Ginger disappears into her room and in a matter of a few seconds shows up back in my room. She is wearing nothing from the waist up except her new bra. I try not to show my embarrassment at seeing her this scantily clad. I know that she sees the bra as an important milestone on the road to full womanhood but I also know how important it is for her to be respected as an adult even if she does come in a small package.

I manage to say, "Nice bra kid. How about showing me how you look in some of the rest of your new clothes. In fact why don't you take a shower and put on something really nice. We'll go out to the best restaurant in town and have meal fit for a king and his princess."

Ginger turns and is gone in a flash. I get one of the new outfits I bought for myself and take it into the bathroom to take my shower. I want my clothes with me in the bathroom. I've had enough embarrassment for one day. I don't need the kid walking in on me before I am fully dressed.

When both Ginger and I are ready we step out the door and head for the car. As I am about to enter the door I notice a SUV parked across the street. There are a couple of guys sitting in it. Both of them dressed in business attire. It seems to me they are a little overdressed for a small town especially after business hours. I really think no more of it until I notice them pull up and park a few parking spaces down from us at the steakhouse. I don't mention it to Ginger. I can do enough worrying for both of us. She seems much more comfortable now than she did this afternoon.

After the hostess has seated us, and the waiter has taken our order, I try making some small talk with Ginger to keep her mind off of the many weighty thoughts I know are lurking in that pretty little head of hers. I say, trying to keep my voice in as normal a tone as I can considering the fact that I know we are being watched and I am not sure if these guys are friend or foe, "Well, now that you have seen the school, are you still so sure you won't be happy going there?"

Ginger doesn't answer right away and when she does she doesn't answer the question I asked. Rather she says, "Thanks for trying to protect me from worrying but I saw those guys too. Do you think they will do anything when we leave here?"

"I don't know. I am not sure if they are the ones after you or if they are from some agency trying to protect us. So for now I intend to keep my eyes on them and not do much else. I don't think, even as dumb as the guys sent for you have been, that they will try anything as long as we are in town. There would be too many witnesses if they did."

"What do you intend to do about them? We can't just let them follow us around until they find a convenient place to kill us."

"That much we are entirely in agreement on Kid. I am working on a plan right now. When I get it figured out I will let you know. Meanwhile if you have any brilliant ideas you might share them with me. I could use a little help here, you know."

"What about your buddy? You know the one that comes up and stays with you sometimes. I think you told me his name is Jack. Maybe he could help us. If he is a hunter he will have guns.

"That is a good idea. I'll give Jack a call when we get back to the motel. However, I am not sure that Jack has any guns. When Jack and I hunt together we use cameras, not guns."

"Boy some protection you guys are. No guns. What's the matter with guns anyway Old Man?"

"It's not the guns Kid. As far as I am concerned there is nothing wrong with guns. It's the killing that is wrong. I don't even want to kill animals. After all they are part of God's creation too. So I have found no need to have a gun. I am not sure but, from what I know of Jack, I don't think he will have any guns either."

"You eat meat Old Man. I know I just heard you order a steak. Cows are animals. Doesn't not killing animals include cows?"

"Yes Kid, I enjoy eating meat. I know that eating meat means that animals must be killed. It is not the killing of animals for food that concerns me. It is the unnecessary killing of animals that concerns me. It also is the unnecessary killing of people that upsets me. Some of the trackers trying to find us were good men who thought they were out trying to find a lost girl. What if I had shot one of them? Then I would have killed an innocent man even though the result of his finding us would likely have meant our deaths and most likely his death too. Now, if it is evident that someone is trying to kill me, or some other innocent person, I guess I would kill again but only if there is no other way.

After this conversation we sit in silence until our meals are served. Finally Ginger breaks the silence by asking, "Where did you and Jack meet? Was it in Vietnam?"

"No. Jack's tour and one of my tours in Vietnam over-lapped, but we met in the shelter when both of us were trying to get off the streets and put our lives back together. Jack, too, had tried the bottle for comfort and, like me, found no comfort there. Jack had not sunk so far into the bottle as I had, but he too pretty well had to start all over again. He had been a combat photographer in Vietnam. When we got sober he was able to get a job as a newspaper photographer. After a couple years of that he started freelancing some. Now all he does is freelance photography."

Ginger gets a serious look on her face, the kind of look that I have learned to recognize as the prelude to a weighty question. Sure enough the question comes only a second or two later.

"Does Jack live in a cabin in the woods too?"

"No Jack has a nice home in Spokane, Washington. He does most of his nature photographs in the national parks near Spokane. Sometimes he does articles featuring different areas. He has done a couple of features about the area around here. He stays with me when he is seeking good shots for his features. Once in a while he just comes up so we can spend some time together. He did the photos for my first book, the one about life on the street. He has done some shots for a couple of my other books. The truth be known, Jack is most likely a little saner than I am."

The Kid never misses an opportunity to give me a good putdown and she doesn't disappoint me this time either. She looks me in the eye and simply says, "That wouldn't have to be too sane, you know."

After we have completed our dinner and paid the waiter we start out the door. The good dinner and pleasant conversation has caused me to almost forget about the fellows watching us. Reality returns though when we reach the car and I hear the SUV's big engine start.

I check the rearview mirror numerous times as we are driving back to the motel. The SUV follows us at a respectful distance. It is difficult to follow someone without being noticed in a small city where there is so little traffic. It appears they don't try to avoid being noticed.

When I park in front of our room at the motel I see them, whoever them may be, park just across the road. I sure hope they have a miserable night sitting in that thing. I intend to have a good night's sleep in a bed. I don't have too much fear of these guys as long as we are in town.

Ginger and I both enter my room and Ginger turns on the television. I open my cell phone and enter Jack's number. While Jack's phone is ringing, I mutter a prayer that he is not out somewhere on a photo shoot. Sure enough I get his answering machine. "Jack this is John. I need your help. When you get this message give me a call on my cell."

About a half hour after my call to Jack my cell rings. It is Jack.

"What can I do for you John?"

"Jack I don't have time to explain everything to you right now. I will tell you everything when I see you. How soon will that be?"

"If you need me I'll fly out tonight. It so happens that my plane is serviced and ready to go. I was going to Maine tomorrow to do a shoot so I can be there before morning. Is that soon enough?"

"That's great Jack. When you get here I can't come to meet you. I am being followed and I need you to be behind the scenes. That way you will have the freedom of movement that I don't have. What I would like you to do is rent a car and come to my cabin, but don't come by way of my drive. Use the entrance I showed you when we were making your last shoot. You know the road that comes in a few miles north of my cabin. You do remember the road I am talking about don't you?"

"Sure I remember John, but can't you give me an idea of what is going on? My curiosity is killing me."

"Jack there is a girl with me. There is someone trying to kill her and me as well now that I am trying to help her. I don't know who they are or much about them except they have already killed the girl's mother and father as well as a game warden. We have gone to the law, but they are not convinced that this is anything but a local problem. We are getting precious little help from anyone with the exception of the local sheriff. Be careful when you come into my place. I don't know that they might not have surveillance set up there too. You won't be of much help if they know about you."

"See you there in the morning John. I've got to get a move on if I'm going to get there in time to meet you in the morning."

"Thanks Jack and good hunting."

Ginger looks at me with a curious look on her face and says, "What do you mean good hunting. You two aren't going hunting are you?"

"No Kid, good hunting is what Jack and I always said to each other if we thought the other one was about to fall off the wagon. It has just become a way for us to say goodbye to each other now."

"You guys are weird, you know."

"Yeah, you're right about that Kid but it appears that we are about all that you have going for you now so I suggest you be kind to us weird old guys."

"I'll keep that in mind Old Man."

"Go ahead and get ready for bed. I'm going to stay up a while after we turn the lights out and keep a watch on those guys across the street."

In a few minutes Ginger has taken another shower, put on her pajamas and is in bed. I turn out all of the lights and open the blinds. From the big chair near the window I have a perfect view of the two guys in the SUV.

Chapter 17

The Kid and I Go on the Lam

I wake with a start. I am not sure what woke me. Whatever it was it is a good thing that it did. The darkness is starting to give way to early morning light. I take a quick look across the street. The two guys are still there. I hope sleeping sitting upright has given them as big a crook in the neck as it has me. I must have fallen asleep shortly after I sat down in the chair. Ginger is right. Some protection I am for her. Oh well, nothing happened so I guess it is all right that I slept. At least I am rested and ready for the day.

I walk over and give Ginger a gentle shake on the shoulder. She rolls over rubs her eyes and says, "What's going on Old Man. There must be some reason for waking me up before its daylight or do you just get a kick out of disturbing me?"

"I guess it is kind of fun to bug you Kid but it is time for us to get up and get out of here."

"Where are we going anyway?"

"We are going back to the cabin and get a few things."

Before I can say anything else the Kid pipes up with, "You sure like to live dangerously don't you or are you just plain suicidal?"

"Believe it or not I have a plan. Who knows, it might even work. If it does we may live another day. Now get dressed and gather up your things. I would like to be out of here in about half an hour."

While Ginger is gathering up her things and getting ready I go in to the bathroom. It only takes me a few minutes to brush my teeth, run a comb through my hair and shave. By the time I am ready Ginger is standing at the door.

"What took you so long Old Man?"

"That's it Kid. I'm an old man and old men are slow.'

As I am throwing our stuff in the car I notice both of our watchdogs are sound asleep. When I drive by them I honk my horn. Both of them are jolted awake and look as startled as if I had shot at them rather than just honked at them.

"What did you do that for? We could have gotten away from them if you hadn't awakened them. Are you stupid or something?"

"No, it's just that getting away from them isn't part of my plan; at least it isn't right now. Besides, their boss would have been plenty mad at them if they had lost us. You wouldn't want their boss to be mad at them would you?"

"I don't see why not. Their boss is the one that wants us dead, you know. I think I kind of want to make him unhappy."

"Good point and making him unhappy is part of my plan. I just want to wait and make him downright infuriated. If everything works out like I plan we should be able to infuriate their boss and give us a few hours head start on them as well."

I pull in and park near the door of Mommy's Café. The Kid and I stroll in at a leisurely pace as though we have no reason to hurry. After the waitress takes our order and turns to walk away I let out kind of a snicker. The Kid looks over at me and says, "What's so funny anyway Old Man? Let me in on the joke too."

"I was just thinking how comfortable we are in here and how miserable those two guys must be out there. They haven't even had any coffee and we are about to have a fine breakfast."

Ginger snickers too and then she says, "It is funny to think that these guys became what they are so they could have fun. I guess it isn't always fun being the bad guy is it?"

We have a leisurely breakfast. Neither Ginger nor I are in a hurry. Once finished we pay our tab and leave. When I back out and start down the street I can see the SUV pull out of its parking space and start to follow us. I head out of town and pull onto the Interstate. Our pursuers seem content to just follow us for now.

When we exit the Interstate I expect them to try to force us over like Ginger said they did to her mother. They still haven't made a move of any kind when we turn off on the road to my garage.

I drive slowly to see if these guys are going to make their move on us but they seem content to just follow us. They stay well back of us. It appears my plan may work after all. When we reach the point where the drive makes almost a complete U-turn I make the turn then pull over and stop.

"What are you doing Old Man?"

"I don't have time to explain right now. I'll explain later." With this I jump out of the car, open the trunk and grab my bow and four arrows. I run into the center of the U and find a position where I can get a good shot at the criminal's car. My best opportunity will be when they reach the point where they will need to slow to a crawl to get around the turn. I don't have to wait very long before their big, gangly SUV lumbers up to that point. I pull up my bow and let an arrow fling. Bulls eye; the right front tire deflates almost instantly after the arrow enters it. I notch another arrow and fire it into the right rear tire. This shot achieves the same result as my first shot.

I see the right front door fly open. I figure this is my cue to get out of here fast since I expect bullets to start flying around here soon. I am not disappointed. The lead is flying thick and fast by the time I reach my car. The trees are not giving me the protection I was expecting from them. Bullets fly all around me. I am lucky enough to get back to my car and drive away before they hit me. Those bullets must have eyes and steering wheels to get around all those trees. I leave the car in front of the garage grab our gear, including the clothes we bought in town. "Come on, lets get out of here before our friendly criminal types can walk up the drive far enough to get a shot at us."

Ginger doesn't hesitate. She's right on my heels. Just as we reach the steps to my porch I hear the zing of an arrow followed by a loud scream of someone in great pain.

I look over to Ginger and say, "Jack's here."

Ginger, with a look of pure terror on her face, looks up and says, "It's a good thing. That guy had us dead if Jack hadn't gotten him. Where is he anyway?"

"I'm right here," Jack says as he steps from behind a nearby tree and don't be too quick to judge John. We have been giving each other signals since the two of you came into sight."

"Before we do the formal introductions Jack, what is our would-be assassin doing?"

"Oh, he took off limping down the trail toward your garage." Jack says with a note of pleasure in his voice.

"Is he still armed?"

"No, his pistol must have flown fifteen feet away from him when I shot him. He is unarmed now except for my arrow in his thigh. I don't think he has much fight left in him."

"Are there any other guys lurking around here Jack?"

"No, none but the ones that came in with you."

"Okay, I am going into my cabin and grab my computer and a couple of other items and then I suggest we get out of here. Would you mind keeping a watch while I am doing this?"

"You've got it John, but make it fast. I feel a little under armed going up against these guys with guns when all I have is my bow and a few arrows."

As we enter the cabin I am surprised to see my computer still sitting where I left it. Surely they checked it out for any information I might have on it that would be of interest to them.

Oh well, what the heck. I grab it and stick it, along with a few CD's, into its case. I also grab my checkbook and a couple hundred dollars in cash that I had stashed in the cabin. Not knowing who all might be tracking me I will need to devise a way to buy things and keep in touch in such a way that it will not give away our location. While I am having these thoughts I am exiting the cabin by its back door. Of course Ginger has to get her two cents worth in.

"Hey, aren't you forgetting something? Don't you think it would be a good idea to let Jack know we are leaving?"

"Jack knows Kid."

"Now how does he know, is he a mind reader or something?"

"No, Jack's not a mind reader, but he is a combat veteran. In combat situations you learn to use non-verbal means of communicating, sometimes because you can't hear verbal commands and at other times because verbal commands might give away your location. Now if you can carry the computer it will speed up our getting out of here.

Ginger reaches over and takes the strap to my computer case. I am still left carrying both backpacks, both sleeping bags and a trash bag I stuck our new clothes in. It's a good thing we are only going a couple of miles. I'll be lucky to make it that far without stopping for a rest. Right now I don't think stopping for any reason is a good idea. Ginger, not able to contain her curiosity any longer, pipes up with another question.

"Where are we going?"

"Jack has a car up the trail about a mile and a half. We are heading there. Jack will meet us there and take us to a location where hopefully we can drop out of sight. Do you have anymore questions?"

"Yeah, I do. What I meant is where are we going from there?"

"First, it doesn't matter too much so long as we are safe from our pursuers. When we get there our next move will be decided after you and I have a real long heart to heart talk."

"What good will that do? I've already told you everything I know about what is going on. Don't you believe me?"

"Sure I do Kid, but I need to know everything I can about your father, his business, his associates, his last moves, etc. I think you know a lot that you don't realize is relevant to our situation. Now let's cut out the chatter. I am short of breath so I need to use what breath I have for walking not talking. Okay?

We walk on in silence for about half a mile. I take most of our gear and hide it in an outcropping of rocks not far off the trail. We continue walking until Jack's rental car comes into view. Jack is leaning against it waiting for us.

Ginger pipes up with, "How did he get ahead of us? He was behind us when we left."

"He didn't have to use up his breath talking to you Kid."

When we reach Pottersville, I have Jack drop me off a few blocks from the bank. I walk into the bank and write them a check for a thousand dollars. After a great deal of checking out my life's history and a lecture on the danger of carrying so much cash, I finally manage to get the money and leave.

I walk down the street for a few blocks and then turn down a side street. Jack pulls up beside me before I walk much more than a half block.

When I get into the car Ginger pipes up with, "You guys are creepy. You seem to know what each other are going to do without saying anything. Do you ever talk or do you just use this non-verbal communications so no one, including me, knows what is going on?"

"Okay. What do you want to know?"

"Why did you go back up to our cabin? You knew those guys would just follow us didn't you?"

"Yes Kid, I was counting on it. Now they are up there where their cell phone won't work and their car is disabled. This gives us a little time, free of their beady little eyes, to make our escape."

"Oh, Jack is going to take us out of here?"

"Not exactly, we just want to make them think that he has."

"What do you mean by 'not exactly' anyway? You don't mean that we are actually going to stay up there at our cabin do you?"

Before I can answer the Kid's question she comes up with still another question.

"Why don't we just get a car and take off?"

"That's just what I would do if we were only hiding from the guys who killed your father and mother. The problem is, as soon as it becomes evident that we are not where we said we would be, the law will be looking for us too. Because you are with me, they will put out an Amber alert. When they do that every law official and almost every citizen will be looking for us. There is no escape from a network like that."

"What are we going to do then? It almost sounds like we are in an impossible situation. Do you have a plan?"

"Yes, but I can't tell you now. Jack has to be able to tell the authorities everything he knows or they may hold him as an accessory to our crimes. We can't afford for him to know our plan. If he knows too much they will hold him and he won't be able to move about freely. He needs freedom of movement in order to find the information we need to get ourselves out of this mess."

I turn to Jack and suggest that we get out of here before the guys we ditched figure out where we are. With this I climb into Jack's rent-a-car and he starts driving out of town. When we reach the main road Jack looks over and asks, "Which way do you want me to turn John."

"Turn north. You can drop us off at the bus station in Schroon Lake. We will make it on our own from there.

Then I turn to Ginger and say, "Okay Kid, we need to know everything you know about your father's business."

"I told you I don't know anything about his business."

"Do you know the name and location of his business?"

"Yes, I do know that much. It is Rodriguez Aviation, in New York City."

"I turn to Jack and ask. Did you get that Jack?"

"Yeah, I got it and I know what I need to do. My question is how am I going to get in touch with you?"

"You don't. I will get in touch with you. We can't risk your being considered as an accessory to our crimes. There are two people you can trust. Tell them everything you know and everything you find out."

"Who are these people?"

"They are Sheriff Chuck Hadley in Glen Falls and Mary Lipski. Mary is a caseworker with Children and Family Services. I am hoping that by you telling them everything it will keep you from being considered an accomplice."

By this time we are at the bus station. I say, "Okay Jack, let us out here, Watch us go into the bus terminal and then drive off. I'll contact you in a couple of days. Any Questions?"

Jack's answer is just what I expect it to be. "No, I think I've got your plan."

CHAPTER 18

WE GET OURSELVES SOME WHEELS

Ginger and I walk into the bus terminal and just stand there for a few minutes. I over-hear an old woman talking to a person who I guess is her grandson. She is telling him that she is short of the money needed to buy their bus tickets to Springfield, Missouri. I go to the ticket window and purchase two tickets to Tulsa, Oklahoma. I walk over to the old lady and tell her that we bought these tickets but we have changed our minds and no longer intend to make the trip. I hand her the tickets. Then I take Ginger by the hand and we walk out of the bus terminal. By the time we accomplish all of this I figure Jack has had time to get far enough away to be unable to see us leave.

Ginger has managed somehow to keep her mouth closed through all of this, but as soon as we are out of earshot of anyone she can no longer keep silent.

"What's going on? Let me in on our plan. Why did you by bus ticket if you didn't intend to use them anyway? Where are we going now? We can't just walk out of here you know. Why did we leave all of our things up on the mountain anyway?"

"Are you out of questions Kid? If you are, I will try to give you some answers."

"Yeah Old Man, I think it's time you give me a few answers. If letting me in on things don't cramp your style too much."

"Not at all Kid. I bought those tickets using a check so the authorities will be able to find that we bought bus tickets to Tulsa. I gave them to the old lady and boy so the tickets will get used. I bought them to Tulsa knowing that the old lady and boy are going to get off in Springfield. This should keep the authorities busy checking for a while. Oh, they'll figure it out but I hope by the time they do we will be tucked away safely in our hide away. As far as where we are going is concerned, we are heading to a sports vehicle dealer down the street a couple of blocks. I am going to buy us some wheels. The two wheel kind. From there we are going back to the mountain except we are going in from the north side not the south side. I hope this will keep the trackers confused enough that they won't find us. I left the gear up on the mountain because I knew we would never be able to carry it on the motorcycle. I think I have answered all of your questions, but if I haven't just hold them until we get back to the mountain and don't say anything while I am dealing for the bike. Okay?"

Ginger agrees to hold her tongue just as we are about to enter the lot. The owner greets us as we come in.

"I would like to see your trail bikes please," I say, trying not to sound too desperate, which is not too easy to do since all I want is to get out of here and back up on the mountain. I guess the mountain has kind of become my security blanket."

"Sure mister. Don't get too many calls for bikes this time of the year. Most people are looking for snowmobiles now. Just follow me over this way."

He leads us across the showroom to where he has several new bikes on display. Then he says, "Are any of these, what you have in mind mister."

"Not exactly, you see my granddaughter and I are up here visiting relatives and I want to show her some of the scenery in this area. You know the scenery that you don't see unless you go out into the midst of it. I don't intend to use the bike much so I was looking for a dependable used bike. Do you have anything like that available?"

"Sure do mister. My mechanic just bought a new bike from me and I took his old bike in on trade. Nobody takes care of a bike like he does. It'll be a good buy for you."

After seeing the bike and doing a little bartering we come to an agreement and I purchase the bike, as well as two helmets. When he starts filling out the paperwork I hand him Jack's driver's license to use as identification. I see a questioning look on Gingers face. Somehow she manages to keep silent, but I knew a question was coming when we were alone. Time is passing and I sure would like to get out of here. Who knows, the authorities may already be looking for us.

Finally, we get all the business handled. The kid and I put on our helmets and leave. It has been a while since I have ridden a trail bike and, to say the least, I am a bit rusty. Another problem is this bike is not street legal so we may get picked up before we make it to the mountain. For this reason I take the first back road we come to. I am immensely relieved to be off the main road. Besides, a trail bike is not built for comfort and is even less comfortable when carrying two. After a great deal of riding we finally reach the trail going up the mountain. I am familiar with this trail, but I don't expect the trackers will be looking for us to come in to the area from this far north. I hope they fall for our ploy of traveling out of the area.

Ginger holds on to me so tight that it is almost painful. She says nothing. I suspect she has never been on a bike before. I think she is scared stiff but she has too much grit to admit it. By early evening it becomes evident that we are not going to make our destination before dark. Trail bikes do not have lights. It makes little difference that they don't. It would be tantamount to suicide trying to ride these trails in the dark. I stop the bike and get off. Ginger gets off too.

"What are we stopping for? Surely this isn't our final destination, is it? Ginger asks with a note of disgust in her voice.

"No, we are not at our destination yet, but it is going to be dark soon. I think we will spend the night over under that rock outcropping. It will give us some protection from the wind."

"What is this anyway Old Man another one of your miscalculations."

"I guess you could call it that. I sure never planned on spending the night on the trail, but I guess we'll have to make the best of it."

"Have you made any more miscalculations Old Man?"

"Yeah Kid, I sure have. We are going to run out of gas before we make it to our destination."

"Just where do you think you are going to get more gas. We are up in the mountains, you know."

"I know. I knew that we would run out of gasoline but, believe it or not, I have a plan."

"You know it would make me feel much better if you would let me in on your plans. It's not that I don't trust you. I just know how forgetful old people are."

At first Ginger's statement makes me mad but seeing the truth in it makes it funny. I laugh and this brings a snicker from Ginger. I am glad. Laughing is good therapy and we can use some good therapy right now.

"I'm sorry. My poor planning means we are going to spend a miserable night out here. I hope I can do better tomorrow. About a mile uphill from my cabin is an old abandoned cabin. This is where I plan for us to stay at least until we decipher the rest of your dad's note. I figure we have about three miles yet to go before we get to it. If my calculations are right the location where we abandoned our gear is about five hundred yards straight down from where we are. All of this doesn't matter much now because it is too late for us to make it to either location before darkness sets in. That's my plan Kid for whatever it is worth."

"Hey Old Man, you may be old, forgetful and sometimes aggravating, but you are all I have. My family couldn't be bothered with me. The authorities think I am just a spoiled brat with too much imagination. The great educators aren't smart enough to tell how educated someone is by talking to them. As for the social services people, all they want to do is to take me away from the only one who is keeping me from getting killed. So no matter how bad your planning may be, no matter how forgetful you are and no matter how aggravating you can be you are stuck with me. Okay?"

"That's fine with me Kid. Now come with me and we'll see if we can find some shelter under that outcropping."

Ginger follows me as I make my way through the underbrush to the rock outcropping. We will be out of the direct line of wind under here, but the rocks are wet and we don't have anything to keep us dry. I am not too sure I don't prefer being in the wind to have the seat of my pants wet. After a little searching around I find a log that will fit nicely under the outcropping and will keep our tails dry. At least the rock we will be leaning against is pretty dry.

Ginger has not said anything since we left the trail. I think she is too pooped to say much. I sit down on the log and Ginger sits down next to me. I put my arm around her and pull her close to me. "We are going to need to stay pretty close tonight so we can share our body heat. After all, that is all the heat we are going to have."

Ginger says nothing. She just nods in agreement cuddles up to me as tightly as she can. We sit there for some time neither one of us saying anything. To say the least, this is a miserable place to spend the night, but it isn't long until Ginger is asleep. I don't have any idea how long I sat there before I fall asleep too. I wake up once or twice during the night, but I cannot see my watch without moving my arm and I am afraid moving my arm will wake Ginger so I just go back to sleep. Finally Ginger wakes me and says she is too cold to sleep. I see what she means. Now that I am awake I realize that both of us are shivering rather violently. It is still too dark to try to walk out of here or even do much to exercise so we can increase our body heat. I curse the misjudgments I made yesterday, but there is little I can do about them now. I just pull Ginger close to me and rub her back and arms trying to gain a little heat for us, by the friction this creates.

Finally dawn starts to break As soon as there is enough light for us to move about I start going downhill toward our gear. Ginger is hot on my tail. There is no trail for us to follow so we have to make our way through the undergrowth.

Finally we reach our gear, which incidentally was not directly below us as I had calculated, but was some two hundred paces back down the road. By now the exercise of walking has warmed us enough that we are no longer shivering.

"Hey, are you ready to start up to the cabin or do you want to rest awhile first, I ask after noticing the tired look on Ginger's face?"

"I'm alright. You just lead the way. I want to get out of here. I feel just a little bit exposed down here on this road. After all, this is the path you left for those guys to follow yesterday, you know."

"You're right Kid. Hopefully they will be so intent on following the tire tracks that they won't notice the footprints we are leaving all over the place."

"Unless they are even more lame-brained than I think they are they should have been past here yesterday," Ginger says with an air of smugness in her voice. Then she adds, "But just in case they aren't that smart I'm for getting out of here now."

I just nod in agreement with Ginger and start looking for a trail we can follow. Now that we are going uphill and carrying our gear it is going to be very difficult for us and I don't think we can manage traveling through the undergrowth. I find a trail and by noon we are almost back to where we abandoned the motorcycle. At this rate we may not make it to the cabin by nightfall. We have stopped every few dozen yards to rest. Ginger is just too much of a lightweight to carry much without stopping for rest at relatively short intervals. I have tried to balance the load between us so that I am in need of rest as often as Ginger is. Sometimes I need a rest break even before she does.

When we get back to where we abandoned the motorcycle, I decide to scale our load down to increase the likelihood of our getting to the cabin by nightfall. I can come back later to pick up the things we will not need tonight. I hide the motorcycle the best I can and leave one pack and the sack of extra clothes. I grab the little black bag I have been carrying and add it to the pile of items to be taken. I notice a curious look on Gingers face and just know as sure as the world is round there is a question coming. I am not disappointed.

"What's in that little black bag anyway?"

"That is my second line of defense." I'll show you someday when we have a little more time on our hands. Okay?"

"Okay. I'll let you keep your secret for now. Speaking of secrets how did you get Jack's drivers license anyway?"

"I found it on the seat when he was driving us to Schroon Lake. I picked it up and slipped it in my pocket thinking that my using Jack's identification might cause more delay in our being found. I sure hope I don't get Jack into trouble."

By the time Ginger is finished with her sentence I am already heading up the trail. With the lighter load and the fact that we are now going on less than a direct line uphill we are both requiring less frequent rest stops. After a couple of rest stops I pull out some beef jerky for us to eat while we keep moving. We make it to the cabin shortly past mid-afternoon.

Ginger takes one look at the cabin and says, "you don't mean to tell me that you plan on us staying in this dump, do you?"

"It's no palace, but it is some shelter and I think we are safe here for a while. With any luck we won't need to stay here too long."

Chapter 19

Home Sweet Yuck

Ginger gives me this look like a professor gives a student whose actions he does not approve. I know it is coming so I brace myself for the oncoming assault and it comes with her very next breath.

"Hey Old Man, why is it that you have been so careful to cover our tracks before and now you just don't seem to care. We've been leaving tracks that a city slicker could follow ever since we left Schroon Lake. You even left the bike right next to the trail. It's almost as though you don't care anymore. If this is an attempt at self-destruction you can leave me out of it. I want to live! Okay?"

"You're right Kid. I told you I would keep you posted as to my plan and I haven't updated you for a while. My idea was to leave a clear set of tracks away from our cabin and into Pottersville and then to Schroon Lake. I tried to leave tracks from the bank to the bus station hoping this would sidetrack everybody looking for us, at least for a short time. This being the weekend should give us a couple of days before the authorities realize that we are missing. Then, with luck, maybe the false trail we left will delay them for a day or two. I intend to leave another false marker for everybody, good guys as well as the bad guys to follow."

"You had better do something Old Man. As soon as that motorcycle sales guy sees the Amber alert he is going to call the cops and they are going to know that we took to the hills rather than going on a bus ride. Just how do you plan to leave another false marker anyway?"

"That's where the bike comes in. If I use my cell phone they will be able to track it to the tower its signal came in from. I intend to let this work to our advantage. They will figure this pin points our position. In order to turn this problem into an asset, I will make each call to Jack from an area that is covered by a different cell tower. Hopefully this will lead them to think we are traveling rather than staying in one place. One problem, though, I didn't take into consideration is the fact, that trail bikes have such small gas tanks. I need to devise a way to carry extra gas with me if I am going to make it to and from these locations."

"I think you had better come up with a plan to get some gas in the first place. We ran out of the stuff, you know."

"I am well aware of that. I have some thirty-gallons of gas back in my generator shed. It is only about a mile from here so I intend to go down and get a couple of five gallon cans."

"Are you nuts Old Man? Don't you think they will be watching your cabin?"

"I suspect they may be but I learned a few things about infiltration of the enemy's position in Nam. I intend to put that knowledge to good use."

"Your plan is making me nervous. I just hope it works."

"You're right. I am relying too much on things happening as I have planned for them to happen. We need to develop an early warning system so we will know if anyone is approaching us. Why don't you put your devious little mind to work on coming up with a system while I am getting the cabin set up for our occupancy."

I expected Ginger to make some kind of a crack about the assignment I have given her, but she says nothing more. She just started walking around outside the cabin. I walk into the cabin and start looking around. I've been up to this old cabin several times, during the years I have lived in this area, but this is my first time to enter it. I can't see daylight anyplace through the roof. This doesn't necessarily mean the roof is watertight, but at least it is a good sign. It has only one room. There is a fireplace at one end of the room. Other than this it is completely empty. I check the fireplace chimney. It appears to be intact enough that having a fire in it will not set the cabin ablaze. The door opens and closes, but the latch is broken. When you close the door it just falls open again. I can fix that by putting a log next to it so it won't hang open all night. The windows are intact, but the shutters are of little use. At least one hinge is broken on each of them.

I spread out our sleeping bags and open a can of potted meat. Our dinner will be potted meat on crackers. I am so tired that I don't even feel hunger right now. I step outside to call Ginger in for dinner. She is sitting on a rock not far from the cabin door. She looks too pooped to move. "Come on in Kid. I fixed us some dinner and laid out our sleeping bags."

Ginger just stands up and starts toward the door without saying a word. When she gets into the cabin she heads straight toward her sleeping bags.

"I know you are tired Kid, but you really need to eat"

Ginger turns and comes over to where I have set out the food. After I say grace, she eats a few crackers with a thin layer of meat spread on them. When she finishes this she goes over and crawls into her sleeping bag without saying a word. When Ginger says nothing you know she is tired. Dead tired!

I get my laptop out and set it up. It is getting dark enough now that I have to use the flashlight to see. After I have it up and running I bring up my spreadsheet software. I wish I had some software designed for deciphering codes, but I guess I will have to make do with what I have available to me. I am not in much of a position for going on a software shopping trip right now.

I pull out the paper with the cipher and start looking at it. I want to see if I can find any clues as to where I might start deciphering it. From the size of the numbers it is evident it is not a simple code where the numbers 1 through 26 equal the letters A through Z. The numbers range from 15 through 58 this is 44 numbers so it can't be that a single number equals a single letter, at least not in sequence. I count the numbers used in the remaining portion of the cipher. There are 25 different numbers used. This makes it evident that there is likely more than one step in the code. There are 17 numbers used only once and there is only one number used more than 4 times. There are only 8 numbers used multiple times. Since vowels are used much more than consonants, the subtraction of 6 vowels would leave only 2 constants used more than once in this statement. I don't feel this is very likely. I think I will work on the theory that Ginger's Dad used at least two codes combined for this message. Of course it could be the reason there are 25 numbers used is because not all letters of the alphabet are used in this message. On the other hand, in this short a message, it is doubtful that 25 of the 26 letters would be used. Oh what the heck. Ginger has the right idea. It's time to get some sleep. I shutdown my computer having not made a single entry on the spreadsheet I had opened. As I am crawling into my sleeping bag I think, all I have accomplished is figuring out a lot of maybes about the code and I have given myself a dilly of a headache in the process.

The problem is, as tired and sleepy as I am, I cannot turn my mind off. I keep reviewing all the possible combinations that Ginger's father could have used for setting up his code. I finally fall asleep only to wake up every couple of hours the remainder of the night. Finally I wake up to find the sun shining in through every opening in the not so tightly sealed old cabin. I rise up, on one elbow, and start to say something to Ginger. I am struck with a sudden attack of fear when I notice that her sleeping bag is empty. Ginger is gone.

I jump up as fast as my aching old body allows me to do so. I rush across the room and look out the door. Ginger is nowhere in sight. I go back to my sleeping bag and retrieve my coat and boots. When I have these on I again rush to the door only this time I go on through and outside. I stand for a while listening to see if I can hear any noise that might indicate which way I should go to start looking for Ginger. As I am standing straining my ears to hear anything there might be to hear I feel a small hand slip itself into my hand. The hair on the nape of my neck flies straight out and I must have jumped half-a-foot straight up in the air.

I look around to see Ginger standing beside me. There is no look of concern on her face. "What are you doing Kid?" I ask trying to shield the concern I am feeling from being evident in the sound of my voice.

Ginger's answers with logic I cannot argue against. "I was just doing what you told me to do Old Man. I was setting up an early warning system for us. You know, so we can tell if we have intruders in the area."

"Okay Kid, but in the future don't go away from me without our discussing it first. Okay?"

"Okay, but I wasn't afraid. I can take care of myself." Then she adds the "you know" onto the end of her statement again mocking my habit of using this expression at the end of my statements.

"Maybe you weren't scared Kid, but I was. We need to watch each other's back and that's a fact."

"Okay," Ginger says looking like she had never considered that she might be protecting me too.

"What kind of an early warning system are you making," I ask with a feeling of curiosity flying around in my head.

"Well, I gave a great deal of thought to how I could make an effective early warning system given the limited resources we have to work with. Finally I thought, what do we hear when we are walking though the forest. We hear twigs snapping. So I found as many dry twigs as I could and spread them out on all the trails around here. I left spaces between the twigs so we can walk without stepping on them. We may not want everybody knowing where we are walking, you know."

"Pretty smart thinking. Now why don't we go in the cabin and have something to eat. After we eat I need to go down to my cabin and get us some gasoline"

Before I am hardly finished making my statement Ginger pipes up with, "I'm going too."

"No! It is just too dangerous. You had better stay here."

"We need to stay together. We need to watch each other's backs, you know"

It makes me mad to have my own words thrown back at me, but it is hard to argue against your own logic and stay creditable so I don't even bother to try.

We go into the cabin together and I forage through our packs to see if I can find something we can eat for breakfast. I fear I didn't pack too much that is appetizing for breakfast. We finally settle on a can of prepared meat. Not one of my favorites for any meal and definitely not for breakfast, but the Kid needs to eat so I let her select. It serves me right for being so nice. I intend to steer clear of this kind of action in the future.

While we are eating the Kid engages her mouth again and out pops another question I would really rather not answer. "You told me you wrote a book about life on the street. Were all of those people alcoholics too?"

"No Kid. There are most likely as many reasons for people to be on the street as there are people on the street. You can put them into categories, I guess. Categories such as alcoholics like me, drug users, people with mental problems, families which can't afford shelter, people with no one who cares. The list goes on and on.

"Why don't they just go get help like you did and get off of the streets?"

"What's with all of these questions anyway Kid? Are you going to write a book?"

"Why not Old Man, you did, didn't you?"

Ginger's response brings a grin to my face. Then I continue trying to answer her question. "I'm sorry to disillusion you Kid, but it is just not that simple. Alcoholism and drug use are addictions. It is very difficult to overcome the body's craving for these after it is addicted to them. Even with the best help available only a few manage to overcome their addiction. Even when successful, many find themselves in the same situation I found myself in. Their loved ones may have died or moved on to other relationships. The mentally ill are in an even greater predicament. Years ago they just locked them up in institutions. Some responded to treatment but those who did not were deprived of their freedom even though they had committed no crime. Most of these people prefer living on the streets to being locked away. I can't say I blame them. I think I would feel the same way if I had their problem. Many are on the streets because they lack the means to get off of them. These often include children. I think they are the saddest of all. The children are there not because of illness or any fault of their own. They are there because of the failures of adults. Now we need to stop all of this talking and get busy trying to get ourselves out of the predicament we are in."

"Okay. What are we going to do?"

"I am going to go down to my cabin and get some gasoline out of the generator shed. You had better stay here where you'll be safe. I wouldn't want a mistake on my part to put you in danger."

"No way, Old Man! I need to go along to make sure nothing happens to you. If they get you, then I am as good as dead anyway. Besides, you agreed to my going before breakfast."

"Okay you win. You can go with me, but only part way. Two people are twice as likely to make a noise or be seen as one. We will hide you where you can observe me but are not likely to be seen if I am seen. Okay?"

"Okay."

I grab the little black bag that I have been carrying, as well as my bow and quiver, the latter of which is holding the few arrows I have left. When I start off toward my cabin Gingers falls right in step behind me. We find it difficult to walk on the trail without stepping on the dry sticks Ginger spread over the trail as part of our early warning system. Thankfully, she only spread them for a few dozen yards down the trail.

We walk for a good hour or so before reaching an area above my garage. From here we can look down on the garage without likely being spotted ourselves. At this point I motion for Ginger to remain where we are. I start walking down toward the garage. I move with as much stealth as I can. It seems that I was not built for sneaking up on anyone. My big feet seem to find every dry twig in the area. I am lucky however. There is no one and no cars near my garage or in my drive.

I make my way back up to where I left Ginger. When I get there I can't find her. "Okay Kid enough of the funny business. We need to get a move on."

With this Ginger steps from behind a tree and follows me as I follow a trail that will bring us out above my cabin. Once there, we hide and watch to see if we observe anyone or anything which might indicate the presence of anyone nearby. After nearly half an hour passes without our having observed anything I open up my black bag and remove my slingshot and a couple of the marbles I keep in it.

Ginger says nothing, but I see the look of curiosity on her face. I load one of the marbles into my slingshot, draw back and let go. I don't hit where I had aimed because the marble clipped a tree which diverted it from my intended target. It does however; hit the side of the cabin. The noise it makes is loud enough that I am able to hear it plainly. We wait for some time, but we see no indication that anyone is nearby. I reload my slingshot and fire a second marble. This time I hit my intended target. It is the galvanized tub, sitting on my back porch. The noise this makes is loud enough that even a deaf person would feel the vibrations of the sound. We observe nothing after this shot either. Either there is no one around or they are wise enough not to fall for my ploy.

I motion for Ginger to remain in place as I start slowly moving from tree to tree toward the generator shed. When I finally reach the back porch I step upon it using care to be as quiet as I can. Then I walk across the wooden sidewalk I built between the porch and the generator shed. The gasoline is still here, somewhat to my surprise. I grab two full five-gallon cans and the nearly empty two-gallon can I keep for my chainsaw and trimmer, and head back outside. Just as I am about half way across the sidewalk I hear voices. This sends a chill up my spine and stands the hair on the back of my neck straight out. It sounds like the voices are coming from the front of the cabin.

I take off as fast as I can, considering the load I am carrying. The trip back up the hill, to where I left Ginger is uneventful, but slow due to the weight of the gasoline. I glance back behind me several times but see no one. As I walk past Ginger she falls in behind me. I reach back and give her the two-gallon can to carry. The trip back up to our hideaway would be hard enough without the somewhere around eighty pounds of gasoline I am carrying. We stop every few dozen yards to rest and allow me to catch my breath. All those years of being a heavy smoker has taken its toll on my lungs I fear. The extra few pounds I have put on add to the burden on my lungs as well. I need to get myself in shape. At several of our stops I find and lay small limbs across the trail trying to make it look like the trail has not been used for a while. This won't fool a good tracker, but I figure that the stooges looking for us won't be smart enough not to fall for our ploy. I don't think they will be using any real trackers now. It would be too risky for them to do so.

It is well past noon when we get back to our hideout. I am pooped and hungry. I decide hunger is the greater problem now. After I catch my breath, I open a can of fruit and a can of potted meat. This, with some crackers, is our lunch. We eat without much conversation. I think the Kid is pretty well pooped out too.

I had planned to go down to where we left the bike and our other gear but I am too tired to do so today. I finally decide my time might best be spent working on the code to see if I can get it figured out before I call Jack. I am anxious to hear what Jack has found out about Ginger's father. Tomorrow will be the last day before the authorities realize that Ginger and I are missing. At least I hope it will be.

I really didn't want to make my first trip before it is known that we are missing. This idea of misleading the authorities by the location of my calls will only work for a few calls. Even if I am successful, sooner or later they will be able to guess our location. I intend to use cell phone towers south of us. By doing this I hope to keep them looking to our south. Anyway, there are not very many towers north of us.

Chapter 20

Things Start Falling into Place

I walk into the cabin and grab my laptop case. I have a notebook and pencil in one of the compartments. To keep the use of our batteries at a minimum I will develop a spreadsheet strategy on paper before I start setting up the spreadsheet on my laptop.

There are an almost endless number of combinations that Ginger's father could have used and now I have to try to get into his head to figure out how he set up his code. I try to pick up my thinking where I left off yesterday. Judging from Ginger's level of intelligence I can assume her dad was an intelligent man, but what could his motives have been for keeping this information hidden? Why would he put his wife and daughter in danger by giving it to them? Was he involved in something illegal?

Enough of these questions! They are not helping me figure out his code. He must have meant for it to be deciphered, just not too easily deciphered. I will try using the code he used for the first part of the message and just add more codes to it. After doodling on the first sheet of the pad I lay it aside and bring up my laptop. I open the spreadsheet and make one row from A to Z numbering the cells to fit the code of the first part of the message. I figure the words "key here" must somehow be the key to his second code, but how? I number the second row with the numbers representing the words "key here', repeating it over and over until I fill in the 26 positions.

I then set up formulas to add the" key here" numbers to the original code in sequence. After completion of the formulas it is quite evident that the numbers are too small to fit the numbers in the second coded section. I add a third row and start trying other possible codes for letters. I start with the letter "A" equal to 26, and then follow in sequence until I reach "Z" equal to 1. This makes the numbers large enough and they even look logical. I will only try to decipher the first word. After a couple of hours it is evident that I cannot make a word out of the numbers I have used. By now it is getting dark and Ginger, who has spent most of the afternoon adding to her early warning system, has comes inside.

"Hey Old Man I'm hungry. What's for dinner anyway?"

"I don't know Kid. Why don't you look in the backpack and fix us something for dinner."

It doesn't take me long to decipher what she has selected. No more than a second or two after I hear her pull the can tab and I smell kippered herring. We sit in silence while we eat this gourmet meal of kippered herring and crackers. We wash it down with bottled water. Boy, this way of living stinks on several levels.

The combination of not getting much sleep last night, combined with the long walk, and all the brain strain of working on deciphering the code has made me sleepy. Add being sleepy to it being dark as pitch outside and I climb into my sleeping bag.

I awake with a start. It is daylight. I must have fallen off to sleep almost as soon as I laid my head down. At least I remember nothing after that until now. A quick glance over toward Ginger's sleeping bag brings me to fully awake. Ginger is gone! I jump up and head for the door. A thousand horrifying thoughts are running through my head as I look through the door and find her nowhere in sight. About that time I feel a tug on my coat sleeve. In my state of high tension I nearly jump to the ceiling.

Ginger calmly says, "Breakfast is ready."

I am so relieved to see Ginger that I instinctively grab her and give her a big hug. After I regain my composure, I walk with Ginger back over to where she has prepared our breakfast. We eat in silence. I am not sure what Ginger is thinking. As for myself I am trying to list everything we need to do and then arrange them in the most logical order. I need to talk to Jack. In order to do that I need to gas up the motorcycle and figure out a way to attach a spare gas can to it so I am not so limited on the distance we can travel. We need to gather some firewood. The weather has been milder than normal so far this year but we can't count on it staying that way. I need to finish deciphering the last part of Ginger's father's note. By tomorrow morning the authorities will realize we are gone and traveling with Ginger will be much more dangerous. That's the whole list, in order. We'll take a trip today. We will go to the first cell tower I have selected. Who knows, maybe something Jack has learned will help me in some way, decipher the code. The more I know about the guy the more I can understand his way of thinking. I guess Ginger has been giving thought to the same things. Anyway she is the first to speak.

"Hey, don't you think it is about time we pick up our clothes. We may not have much of a way to take a bath, but at least we could put on some clean clothes. Another thing, maybe we should talk to Jack to see what he has found out." Then after a few seconds hesitation she says, "Maybe Jack has learned something that will help us get out of here."

"I am in full agreement with you Kid. Grab that small gas can. I will take one of the big ones."

Ginger grabs the two-gallon can and falls in right behind me. We start down the trail toward the bike. I am carrying one of the five-gallon cans. In a short while we reach the place where we hid the bike and our other belongings. The trip downhill sure went faster than the trip up day before yesterday. I guess we were pretty worn out then. Most likely we will be again when we get back this evening. I gas up the bike and then fill the small gas can. With the rope, from the backpack, I lash the gas can onto the fork of the bike letting it rest on the front fender. Ginger and I put on our helmets and I crank up the bike. Ginger climbs on behind me and off we go. After about an hour of bouncing down the trails I note the gas can is getting loose and is in danger of falling off. I stop and climb off the bike. Ginger climbs off too. She starts rubbing her backside with a look on her face like she is surprised to find it still attached to her body. I know the feeling. After about ten minutes of rest and my successfully lashing the spare gas can back to the fork, we take off again.

After another couple of hours of riding we are nearly at an end of out gasoline in the bike's tank. The problem is we are not yet at the point I wanted to reach before making my call. Oh well, I have a good signal on the cell phone so we will just call from here. I will need to devise a way to carry more gas next time out. I enter Jack's cell phone number. While it is ringing I keep my fingers crossed that I get Jack and not his voice mail.

"Hello, this is Jack"

"Hello Jack, this is John. What have you found out so far?"

"I went to Ginger's father's business. It's pretty well shutdown now. I did manage to talk to the mechanic who did most of his work. He was able to give me some information that may be of help to you. He said that Carlo, that's Ginger's father's name, had replaced the engines in his plane with larger engines and had built-in spare gas tanks. He said this had increased the speed and range of his plane. Either he doesn't know how much this increased his speed and range or he was reluctant to tell me. I am not sure which it was. Have you busted Carlo's code yet?"

"No, not yet Jack, I have been working on it but I haven't made much progress. Have you learned anything else about Carlo that might be of help to me?"

"Not too much John. He was a smart man. Everyone tells me that and he was crafty. I have the feeling that he may have been involved in something illegal though."

"Have you let Mary and Chuck in on what you have found out so far?"

"Yes, I have. In fact I am with them now. Would you like to talk to them?'

"No, just let them know that we are all right and we will be seeing them as soon as we feel it is safe to do so. That part in Carlo's message about "and government officials" doesn't do too much for my putting my trust in anyone but the three of you so we are trying to avoid everyone else until this is over. I will get back to you soon Jack. Goodbye for now and good hunting."

With the completion of our call I gas up the bike and off we go heading back to our home, sweet home. We bounce and bump up the trail over sticks, stones and heaven only knows what else. About a half an hour's ride from where we started the bike engine sputters a couple of time and dies. I know almost before I look that we have run out of gas. I hadn't taken into consideration the fact that we were riding uphill much more on our return trip than we had on our trip out. Of course this fact isn't lost to Ginger.

"Hey Old Man, you miscalculated our gas consumption but it's all right with me. I think I prefer to walk. That is if I can still walk after you bouncing us around for the past several hours."

"It is not just walking Kid. We have to push the bike too, you know."

Ginger looking me straight in the eye and says, "You push. I'll cheerlead."

As tired as I am I must admit this was a pretty good comeback. We climb off the bike and I start pushing. Ginger gives me a few words of encouragement but nothing I would consider cheerleading.

Finally, after a couple of hours we get back to where we started. I hide the bike and we gather up the pack and bag of clothes we had left behind on our original trip up to the old cabin.

Neither Ginger nor I say anything as we head back up to the cabin. I keep thinking about the code Ginger's dad wrote. I will try again this afternoon to decipher it. I have been mulling a few ideas around in my head. The problem is there just isn't too much daylight left today.

When we get back to the cabin I ask Ginger, "Will you inventory the food and water we have left? I want to work some on your dad's code before it gets too dark."

"Sure. I need to stand up for a while anyway. I am too sore to sit down."

While Ginger is taking inventory I bring up my computer and remove the third code line. I replace it with another copy of the original code, but in reverse order. I write down the possible letters for each number and shutdown my computer. By the time I figure out that again I have not deciphered the code it is getting too dark to see my paper well enough to continue working.

When I lay my pad down Gingers tells me the results of her inventory. "We have eight cans of meat, some beans, ten cans of fruit, but only 6 bottles of water left."

"Well this means we have only three days of water left if we limit ourselves to one bottle of water a day. We need to find a solution soon or it will be necessary for me to make a trip back to my cabin to get us more supplies.

Ginger sets out a can of potted meet, some crackers and a can of fruit cocktail. As she starts opening the cans she looks over at me and says, "I figure the fruit cocktail will help keep us from being so thirsty. It's the water we are so short on, you know?"

"Yes, I realize that too."

As we sit there eating our supper it suddenly occurs to me that I have never asked Ginger if her dad had given her any information about the code. So I ask, "Ginger did your dad say anything to you about the numbers he wanted you to memorize?"

"No, he never said anything except I was to memorize them. At least that is all my teacher told me about it. He gave the numbers and the instructions to her.'

"Think hard. It may have been something he said to you later or maybe even before your teacher gave you the numbers. It may even have been something he said that didn't make any sense to you at the time."

"No, I can't think of anything he said to me that was out of the ordinary. The only thing I can think of that didn't make sense to me is what Mother told me just before she left me on the trail. I sure couldn't make any sense out of that."

"What did she say? Do you remember?"

"Sure I remember Old Man. I'm smart, you know?" She said," remember this. One is to be expected, two is simple and three repeats itself. Do you know what she meant?"

"I'm not sure, but it sounds like a clue to me. Why didn't you tell me this before?"

"It didn't make sense to me so I figured it wouldn't make sense to you either."

"I am reasonably sure you have a higher IQ than I do but I do have a lot of experience that you have not yet gained. In the future tell me everything. Okay?

"Okay. I'll do that, but right now I can't think of anything I haven't told you."

"Okay. One thing I do know though. I'm too beat to do anything with this new information tonight. I'm going to bed and worry about it again tomorrow. Goodnight Kid."

"Good night Old Man."

I wake up with my heart racing, sweating a cold sweat and my nerves standing on end. I've dreamed that I was back in Nam. The faces of those long ago dead were as plain as if I'd seen them just yesterday. I have no idea what time it is, but one thing is for sure, I am not willing to go back to sleep. I don't feel like I could stand it if I had another dream like that.

I fear the Kid may be having some disturbing dreams too. She keeps mumbling in her sleep and every so often she jumps and twitches around in her sleeping bag. About the time I think maybe I should wake her she sits up and yells out, "Don't let them kill me!"

I extricate myself from my sleeping bag and crawl over to Ginger. She is shaking like a wet dog trying to dry itself. I put my arms around her and pull her tight to me. "It's all right Kid. I am here and nobody else is. You were just having a bad dream."

Ginger reaches over and pulls me even tighter to her without saying a thing. We stay like this for some time before she at last releases me from her grip. Finally Ginger speaks and what she says is troubling.

"What did my dad do that was so bad that so many people want me dead?"

"I have no idea. I can't understand why your father would do something that would put you in such danger. From what I have been told he was a smart man. Surly he knew that giving you information would only put you and your mother in grave danger. I have a hard time believing he could be so callus as to not care."

"If your dad was as smart as it appears he was, then he must have made a plan he expected to protect you and your mother. Tell me everything you can about your father. Maybe if I know more about him it will help me figure out how he thinks. This could be important information for deciphering his code."

Ginger sits silent for a few moments and then she says, "Dad was born in Venezuela. His parents and four brothers still live there. When he was eighteen he took a job on a ship. After he worked on it for a while he ended up in the United States. He became an American citizen by joining the army, I think. Anyway, he learned to fly while he was in the army. He also was taking college courses while he was still in the army. That is where he met my mother. Mom didn't like the military life very well so Dad left the service and started his own business. I think my grandpa gave him enough money to buy his first airplane. I was born about the time he started his business. That's about all I know about Dad. Does any of this help you?"

"I don't know, but between what your mother said to you and what you have told me about your dad I have a few things to think about."

I am not sure if what Ginger's mother told her has anything to do with the code or not. I can't figure out what else it could apply to that would make sense. I figure as frightened as she must have been at the time, she wasn't just telling her daughter a riddle. It must have been something that she thought would help protect her daughter. She must have known that she was about to lose her life, yet she tried to protect her daughter the best way she knew how. She was a brave woman.

All of this thinking is not solving the mystery of the code, though. It is getting light enough that I can see my way about the cabin. Ginger is up now and has fixed us breakfast, if you can call cold beans and fruit cocktail, breakfast. I need to do some serious thinking which means I need to find something for Ginger to do so she won't disturb my train of thought. I know, I will have her gather some firewood. It is much colder now than it was when we woke up. I fear it may start snowing. We are overdue for a good snow. I look over to where Ginger is sitting and say, "How about you gathering us some fire wood. I would like to have a little heat for us tonight. The temperature must have fallen ten degrees since we awoke this morning. I think that is a sign that the milder than normal weather may be coming to an end."

"Sure, I can do that, Old Man."

With this she heads for the door. I hear myself saying, "Be careful out there! We can ill afford for one of us to get hurt or sick. If you get to feeling too cold, come in and warm up for awhile."

"Okay, I'll do that."

Before she finishes her sentence she is out the door and out of sight. I return to the problem of deciphering the code. I think of what Ginger's mom told her. There are three parts to what she said. This, I think, confirms my theory that there are three parts to the code. Now I'll try to see if I can determine what the parts are. "The first is to be expected". This part I would guess is the code he used for the first part of the message. "The second is simple." This part I am not sure of. "Three repeats itself." I am going to figure this refers to the numbers for the "key here" part of the message. I guess I need to set up my spreadsheet with these two codes and then work on what is meant by the "second is simple".

I get my laptop out and put in the first and third codes as I think they are. Then, just as a wild guess, I put in "A" through "Z" as one through twenty-six. This is simple all right. Maybe too simple, but it will do for a first try.

I look at the results and start writing down the possibilities. After about an hour I have come up with a word. I am not sure if it is just an accident or if I am on the right track, but it is encouraging that I have at least been able to finally make a word out of all of this gibberish. The word is "Locker" I start working on the second set of numbers and after another hour or so I have been able to come up with a second word. The second word is "One". I continue working until I have five words deciphered.

I have been so lost in my work that I have given little attention to Ginger. She has been in and out several times. Each time she has come in with an arm load of wood. Suddenly I hear the sound of a twig cracking. This is followed by several more like sounds. I freeze for a moment then I crawl over to the door and peek out through one of the many holes in it. By this time I can hear voices. I only hope Ginger has also heard the noise and has taken cover somewhere. I curse myself for sending her outside while I am crawling over to where I have left my bow and quiver of arrows. I pick them up and drag them with me as I crawl back to the door. By now the men are in sight. There are two of them. I try to see if I recognize them, but I cannot get a good look at either one's face. I finally can hear them well enough to be able to tell what they are saying. What I hear puts fear in me, but all turns out to be okay.

The taller fellow says, "I didn't know there was a cabin up this far. I thought John's cabin was the last one going up the mountain. Do you want to look it over?"

The shorter fellow answers, "Maybe sometime we will do just that, but I think it is high time we start back down. It looks like it could start snowing anytime now and I don't relish being caught up here in a snow storm."

The taller fellow just nods his head in agreement and they turn and start walking back down the trail they had just come up. I breathe a sigh of relief. Then I realize that I still don't know where Ginger is. I stand up from the kneeling position I have been in and open the door just in time because Ginger comes dashing thorough it so fast that I doubt she would have bothered to open it.

"Hey John I thought we were in deep trouble this time. Those guys were right in front of the cabin before they turned back. What happened anyway?"

I know Ginger is really up tight because she called me John and not Old Man. I try to reassure her by saying, "It's all right. They were just a couple of hikers. I don't think they know we are here. They were worried about the weather and decided to start down. Your early warning system worked pretty well, though. If it hadn't been for it, we might have been discovered."

I glance outside the cabin and note the hikers had good reason to be concerned. It is snowing. I fear my good luck with the weather is about at its end. If we get too much snow the trail bike will be of little use to me. That will mean my grand plan for fooling the authorities by calling Jack from different locations will no longer be possible. Oh well, I guess I had best use the time I have left to see if I can finish deciphering Carlo's code.

I don't have much power left in the second laptop battery. I only brought three so I have to use the laptop sparingly. I have five words deciphered. I am not sure if what I have makes sense or not. The first five words are "locker one-one-three greyhound". I continue working on deciphering the code. After another couple of hours and just about the time my second battery for the laptop gives up, I have the entire message decoded. It reads, "Locker one-one-three greyhound terminal Memphis TN."

I need to get this information to Jack as soon as I can. The problem is it is getting dark and it is still snowing. The snow is not coming down quite as fast now and it is getting finer. The other problem is, it is cold in here. As dangerous as it may be I feel we need to build a fire.

Ginger has been sitting beside me during most of the time I have been working on the message. When I lay the paper with the decoded message on it down, Ginger picks it up and reads it out loud. After she has read it she says, more to herself than to me, "What does this mean?" What locker in Memphis. Dad didn't have anything there? Where is the key for the locker?"

"Those are all good questions Kid. I don't know the answers to them either. I was hoping maybe you could help me make some sense out of your dad's message. Do you have a clue to what any of this means?"

"I have told you all I know about my dad. It was almost like he tried to keep me from knowing much about him. I do have a picture of him that I haven't shown you. Do you think seeing it might be of some help?"

"I don't know, but right now almost any clue would help. Do you have the picture with you?"

Without saying a word Ginger reaches into her coat pocket and pulls out a well worn picture and hands it to me. I look at it. It is a picture of a good-looking man, rather slight in build. He is standing next to an airplane. I don't see much that will help so I start to hand the picture back to Ginger then something registers in my mind and I draw the picture back to me. A second look confirms my inclination. Part of the identification number on the plane is 113. I hand the picture back to Ginger, but before I can speak Ginger pipes up saying,

"You have a strange look on your face. Is there something in the picture that may be of help to us?"

"Yeah Kid, I think the answer to at least one of our questions is in that picture."

Ginger looks at the picture for a minute or so and then says, "I don't see anything that answers any of my questions."

"It's there. Look at the identification number on the plane. It has the numbers 113 in it. I think this is where your dad hid the key. I had only considered the part of his message saying "Key Here" to mean the key to his second code and it was, but it may have been the answer to a second question as well. It may have told us where the locker key is hidden. I've got to get this information to Jack as soon as I can."

"Well in case you haven't noticed it is snowing outside and it is starting to get dark too. I don't think this is a very good time to be traipsing about in the woods."

"You are oh, so right. So I guess it is time to start a fire and get something to eat. Right now my old body doesn't know if it is going to expire of hunger or hyperthermia, but both warmth and food are needed, and soon."

Ginger and I set about taking care of these needs. I begin working on starting a fire and Ginger starts pulling food out of the backpacks. In a few minutes we have both a fire and a meal ready. We eat mostly in silence. I have this feeling running up and down my spine like I get when something is going to happen that I would rather avoid. Sure enough half way through our meal it comes and it is whopper. Ginger looks up and says, "Tell me about sex Old Man. I don't mean the stuff in school books about health, but I mean the real life kind of sex. You know what I mean, don't you Old Man?"

I have never given any thought as to how one should explain sex to a preteen girl. This is one of the times a person envies actors with the ability to just fade out of the scene. I guess all I can do is give it my best shot, but first I'll make one last, final effort to get out of doing this. I would much rather a women explain this to her. A women would understand the emotions, the yearnings, the physical feelings, etc How can a man know how it feels to have a period? So I say, "Ginger do we need to talk about this right now? Didn't your mother or your teacher ever talk to you about sex?"

"No. Both of them told me I was too young to be worrying about sex. Do you think I am too young to know about sex?"

"No, I don't think I do. Maybe you are a little young to know all the details, but if you are curious about sex then I think it is better for you to learn about it from someone that cares about you than to learn it from someone who might have ulterior motives. The problem with my telling you about sex is I am not now, nor have I ever been, a girl. I don't know the emotions girls feel. I don't know about the pressures girls feel. I don't know much about how girls develop both physically and emotionally. I think it would be much better if you had your talk with a lady than man."

Ginger looks me straight in the eye and asks, "Why is everyone afraid to talk about sex? It's something that everybody has isn't it?"

"You're right Kid, we are all sexual beings. Another thing you are right about is the proper time to talk about sex is when you are curious about it. So I will try my best to give you an explanation, at least up to a point. On the subject of the anatomy of sex, well, we will wait until we have a good text book that explains it with proper illustrations. Okay?"

"Okay John, if this is what you think is best."

Well, chalk one think up in my favor. She called me John. This is something she only does when she wants to show respect for me. I am not sure where to begin. I guess I will just start talking and see what I say. “Okay Ginger. Sex is something you have from birth. You are born either a girl or a boy. As you are growing up you will enter an age called puberty. At that time your body will begin to develop sexually. I am surprised that your mother or your teacher didn’t explain this to you. Shortly you will begin what is referred to as ovulation. At that time you will experience bleeding from the vagina for a few days once each month.”

At this point Ginger interrupts me saying, “I know about that. What I want to know about is having sex. You know what I mean don’t you?”

“Yes, I know what you mean. Having sex is the joining of the male and female bodies together almost as one. In this way a man and woman show their deep affection for one another. It is a wonderful experience when it is done with love. If love doesn’t exist between the couple then it loses its wonder and just becomes the satisfaction of an urge. The act of sex should be reserved for the love of your life. Sex can be wonderful when it is done as a part of a loving union between a husband and a wife. Otherwise it can be tragic. It can bring about unwanted children; spread social diseases can bring about all manner of unhappy results. Love is too strong an emotion to be lightly treated. I will ask Mary to talk to you about the emotions of being female if you would like.” With this the conversation ends. We both sit in silence for quite some time then Ginger starts readying herself for bed. I am in agreement with her. The events of the day, though not physically strenuous, have been emotionally strenuous and I am tired too. I walk over and add a couple of larger logs to the fire. With the coals that have built up these logs will last us for some time. I pull off my coat and boots then climb into my sleeping bag zipping it up around me.

CHAPTER 21

GETTING THE MESSAGE OUT

I wake up while it is still dark outside. I am not sure what woke me, but I sure don't look forward to crawling out of this snug sleeping bag. The fire has burned out completely. There isn't even an ember left. With great dread I unzip the sleeping bag and crawl out. Thank heavens I had the good sense to put my coat and boots inside the sleeping bag last night. With great haste I remove the ashes from last night's fire. I just pitch them out one of the rear windows. When I return to the fireplace I break up a number of small sticks laying them in random order leaving air space around each one. With all my care it still requires four matches to get them to light. I guess I just failed the Boy Scout requirement of starting a fire with only two matches. After the bulk of the sticks are on fire I add a couple of slightly larger sticks. Each time the sticks I have added are burning well, I add a couple of larger sticks until I have a pretty good fire burning. Even as open as this old cabin is, the fire almost makes its temperature bearable.

By now it is starting to get light outside the cabin. I am almost afraid to look outside. It was still snowing the last I could see last night. One look and I find my fears to be well founded. The snow must be a foot deep, with drifts that may be twice again that high. If the weather could only have held for a couple more days, we would have been able to get the message out to Jack without too much difficulty. Now I have no idea how I can get the word out. I will have to work on figuring out a way, but now that I am warm I realize that I am hungry. I walk over and lay my hand on Ginger's shoulder and give her a gentle shake. Well, so much with being gentle. She doesn't even moan. I give her a rather firm shake while saying, "Wake up Kid. It's time for breakfast."

Ginger moans and rolls over in her sleeping bag. I go over to the backpack with most of the food in it and pull out some tinned meat and some canned fruit. Some breakfast! By now Ginger is up and has her boots on. She walks over to the window and looks outside.

"Holy mackerel, Old Man we are snowed in, but good! How do you intend to get a message out to Jack anyway?

"Good question Kid. Do you have any bright ideas?"

"It appears to me that the only way out of here now is to walk and it doesn't look like that will be very easy."

I don't answer Ginger. I just motion for her to come and get something to eat. We both sit in total silence while we are eating our breakfast. During breakfast I conclude what I have to do. I am not sure how to tell Ginger. I am almost sure that she will protest, but I can't come up with any other ideas of how to get the information out to Jack. Just as I am about to speak Ginger says, "Hey Old Man what's your plan?"

"I have been trying to come up with one Kid. So far the only plan I've come up with is a bad one, but I think it will have to do."

"So tell me. Okay?"

"Okay, here's my plan. I am going to walk up the mountain and hope I can pick up a signal on the top or the other side. I have never been up there so I am not sure that I can make it but somehow we have to get the information we have to Jack. You will have to stay here. There is just no way you can make it through the snow drifts."

Before I can say more Ginger pipes up with a most likely true observation. "You'll freeze your can off out there, you know."

"Most likely true, but as you said we are snowed in pretty good right now and in this part of the country snow that comes now will most likely be here next spring. It will just be under a lot of newer snow. I think we have to make our move now or sit here and wait to see which comes first our freezing to death or our starving to death."

"When you put it that way it makes more sense than I thought it did when you first said it. When do you plan on leaving?"

"I think I better leave as soon as I can get things ready. The odds are pretty good that the weather is not going to get much better so I best get going while I feel I still have half a chance to make it. Conditions for you aren't going to be too wonderful either, you know. Your early warning system is not going to work very well under the snow. You will need to use the remaining fire wood sparingly because it will be near impossible to get more now that it is covered with snow. I suggest you spend as much time in you sleeping bag as possible."

Ginger says, "What if you get yourself killed out there Old Man."

"I'm a pretty tough old bird, you know. I don't think I will get killed, but you are right. We should have a plan just in case something goes wrong. Under normal circumstances I could make the top of the mountain from here in a day and the return trip would take even less time, but with the snow it will make both the trip up and the trip down slower. I also don't know if I will be able to get a signal on my cell phone at the point where I reach the top. I may need to move around a bit to find a place where I can get a signal. You stay here until you are down to one day's worth of food before leaving. When you leave go to my cabin, but make sure no one is there or near there before going too close. Jack knows to check my cabin every few days and, the longer we are out of contact, the more often he will check it. I know you won't be able to identify trails and a lot of landmarks will look different with the snow. To find my cabin from here just go as straight downhill as you can and you should come out close enough for you to see it. I figure you have at least five days worth of food so try not to leave until you are down to one day of food."

With this I stand up and start rolling up my sleeping bag and packing up one pack with what I will need to take with me. Ginger says no more. It is hard to tell if she is just resigned to her fate or if she just doesn't know what to say. Finally I have my gear together and start toward the door of the cabin. Then it occurs to me that my leaving that way will leave foot prints in the area which can be observed by anyone coming up the trail so I turn toward the windows at the back of the cabin. As I am climbing out one window Ginger says, "Don't you die out there, Old Man. I have kind of become fond of you" then she adds the mocking words, "you know."

I about half-climb and half-fall out the window. My sleeping bag gets hung up in the window opening and leaves me hanging with my feet about a foot off the ground. After much shaking and jumping around I manage to free myself and fall the rest of the way to the ground. The snow has drifted up against the cabin such that I am standing in snow waist deep. It takes a Herculaneum effort to move, let alone make forward progress. By the time I have managed to extricate myself from the drift I am almost worn out.

Once I am clear of the drift I have a problem finding the trail going uphill. Not all paths through the trees are trails. I have been walking for what could not have been more than a half an hour and I am so tired that I have to rest. I haven't even made it far enough that the cabin is out of sight. One glance up the mountain and I realize the magnitude of the trek I have embarked upon.

My life is sure one of contrasts. First, I was a husband, a father and a school teacher with a promising future. Then, I was street person, an alcoholic with nothing and no future. When I was in Nam, I thought I was going to sweat myself away to nothing. Now I am about to freeze to death. Life sure takes some strange turns. I have done more with Ginger and I have spent more time with her than I have with either of my own daughters.

Well, I guess I had better start climbing again. I am getting cold. When I climb I get tired. When I stop to rest, I get cold. I must be careful not to exert so much effort that I start to sweat under all these clothes. If I sweat enough to get my undergarments wet, I will be all the colder when I stop to rest. With these thoughts in mind I get up and start climbing again.

Memories of my past life keep floating in and out of my head. I have heard that just before death your whole life flashes through your mind. I hope this isn't what is happening to me. I have such mixed emotions about what I am doing as it is. I don't know what will happen to Ginger if something happens to me and I fear to think of such an event. I don't know if I will be able to get a signal on my cell phone even if I make the top of the mountain. If I do get a signal I don't know if it will be from a tower east or west of the mountain.

I have managed to climb another couple of hundred yards and again I am tired. If I stop to rest this often it may take two days to climb this mountain. With this thought in mind I stop to rest again. The wind has come up making any exposed skin miserable. About all I have exposed are my eyes and the skin adjacent to them, but that is enough to cause a great deal of misery. One good thing about the wind though, it is blowing the snow about enough that my trail is disappearing behind me.

It is starting to get darker. I am not sure what time it is, but I am sure it is not time for it to be getting dark yet. This must mean that I am likely to get caught in some more bad weather. If it snows enough to increase the depth of the snow very much I will be unable to walk in it. With this thought in mind I get up and start climbing again. If I make it to the top I guess I will be able to fall back down the mountain.

My old lungs feel as if they are going to burst. I rue every single cigarette I ever smoked. It is funny how you can regret having ever done something yet have such a craving to do it again. I guess being an ex-smoker is not much different from being an alcoholic. You never get over being an addict you just become a non-practicing addict.

This time I make a little greater distance before completely tiring out. I not only need the rest I need to eat. I find a fallen tree that is mostly above the snow. I sit down on it and remove my pack. To open the pack requires me to remove my mittens. With the mittens removed my fingers become clumsy and then partially useless within a few seconds. I do manage to get some jerky out of the backpack and into my mouth before I have to put my mittens back on. I sit for some time just chewing the jerky and relaxing. I'm not sure that you can ever relax under such conditions but I do my best. The sky continues to grow darker. This is enough incentive for me to get up and start climbing again.

When I was in Nam what I would have given for some of this snow. Now I would love to pack it all up and ship it over there. I guess I need to quit all of this complaining. There is no one here to hear my complaints except me and I am getting tired of listening to them.

Walking has become easier and I am making good time now. The slope of the mountain has leveled off some. Finally my curiosity gets the better of me. I pull my left mitten off and work my shirt sleeve up until I can see my watch. It is two o'clock. No wonder I feel so beat. I have been climbing and resting for nearly six hours now. I will try to make it another couple of hours and then I must stop. Ginger is right. I am an old man and this climbing a mountain in the snow is doing nothing to make me feel younger.

I continue walking for another couple of hundred yards, but the going is getting tougher again. Looking ahead, it appears the slope will soon be so steep that I will not be able to walk. I will have to use the trees to pull myself up. The problem with that is they are not spaced at an optimal distance for doing so. I will have to use the rope somehow. Right now I just can't think of a way to do it. I am so tired I will never be able to do this today. I need to find some kind of protection from the wind and set up camp for the night. It would be nice to find a rock outcropping that would offer me cover, but there is no such thing in sight. The best place I can find within a reasonable distance from the trail is a dead tree leaning against another tree. The lower end of it being on the ground has snow drifted up against it. This will offer me some protection from the wind. Ideally I would dig a snow cave, but this snow is so dry that any attempt to dig a cave into it would be futile. As soon as I would scoop out a hand full of snow the snow above would just fall down and fill in the hole I had dug. I will have to make do with the shelter the tree trunk and snow drift provides.

After much effort I finally reach my goal. As I settle down behind the drift I find I am protected from the wind. This alone makes a great deal of difference in the degree of cold I feel.

I remove my mittens and remove my pack. After removing the sleeping bag and rolling it out I remove my boots and coat. I clean as much snow from my boots as possible then I place, both my coat and boots into the sleeping bag. Once this is accomplished I climb in myself and pull up the zipper. I am so cold that I am not sure I can create enough heat to warm the inside of the sleeping bag. I lay for some time shivering violently before I finally begin to feel warmer and the shivering subsides.

Now that I am getting comfortable I realize just how hungry I am. I don't want to get cold again, but the only way to get something to eat is to unzip the bag and get some more jerky out of the backpack. I lay there for quite some time debating on which would be least painful, starvation or freezing. Finally, hunger wins out and I unzip the bag and get some jerky out of the pack.

After satisfying my hunger, or at least discouraging it, my mind starts giving me misery. All the things that can possibly go wrong start running through my mind until I am in a state of funk. Finally, I decide to say a long prayer and then try to get some rest. I need to be at my best tomorrow if I intend to make the top of this mountain. All the time I have lived here I have never been above the old cabin I left this morning.

"Lord, please grant me the strength to do what is necessary to protect Ginger. I do not deserve your favor, but I call upon your amazing grace to be shed upon me. I ask that you be with Ginger as I know she is lonely and afraid. May thy will be done. Amen."

I am not sure when I fell asleep, but it couldn't have been long after I finished talking to the Lord. It's light. It appears we got no more snow during the night. I must get started climbing. It is lighter now than it was all of yesterday. I unzip the sleeping bag and sit up. After getting my coat and boots on I get some jerky for my breakfast. I always kind of liked beef jerky, but it is a poor substitute for bacon and eggs. Coffee is what I miss most though.

After eating my breakfast and packing up my gear, I put on the backpack and stand up. At least the wind has died down to just a slight breeze. I need to figure out some way to use the rope to help me climb or I won't be able to go much further. As I start to climb over the old tree to get back to the trail I notice a limb about two inches in diameter. If I could break off a piece about a foot or a foot and a half long I could tie it to the rope. I could then throw it into the fork or between two branches on a tree uphill from me. This would anchor it so I could use it as an aid to climb uphill. By doing this enough times I could make the top of the mountain.

My first several attempts at throwing the stick though a fork of a tree are not too successful, but finally I do manage to do so. Even with the aid of the rope it is difficult climbing up this steep slope. After finally reaching the tree in which the rope was hung, I have difficulty freeing the rope so I can use it again. I decide I cannot continue to climb with all of the weight I am carrying so I remove the backpack with the sleeping bag attached and lean it against the tree I just reached.

Again it requires a considerable number of attempts before I manage to get the stick to lodge in the fork of a tree somewhat up the slope from my position. With great effort I continue moving up the slope from one tree to another until I finally reach the top. After removing my left mitten I reach in my pocket and pull out my cell phone and turn it on. I have a signal, but it is not very strong. I decide to walk along the ridge for a ways to see if I can get a stronger signal … I leave the rope hanging from the tree I last used as a climbing aid. This will mark the place where I came up even if the wind comes up and covers my tracks. I must not lose my pack and sleeping bag. It would be sure death if I did.

After walking for a distance of maybe two hundred yards I find the signal has increased. It is still not great, but I doubt that I am going to get a better signal than this. I again remove one of my mittens and enter Jack's number. It rings twice before I hear Jack's voice saying, "This is Jack"

"Jack, this is John. I have the message decoded. Do you have a pencil and pad handy?"

"Just a second John, I will get one." After a couple of seconds Jack says, "Okay John, I'm ready to take down your message."

"Okay, the rest of the message is 'locker one-one-three greyhound terminal Memphis TN'. Did you get that Jack?"

"Yes I got it, but what about a key or a combination so I can get into the locker."

"Ginger showed me a picture of her dad standing by his plane. Part of the number on its tail was one-one-three. I think he hid the key in the plane."

"Good enough John, I will check it out."

"I will get back to you in a couple of days to see what you have found out. Good hunting."

With this I close the cell phone and started walking back to where I had left the rope hanging. I use the rope in my descent by looping it around a tree and then holding both sides, of the rope feeding it through my hands as I slide downhill. I continue to do this until I reach a tree to block my feet against. I then pull one side of the rope until the other side is pulled from around the tree which it had been looped. I do this a couple of times, but find that my sliding speed is not so fast as to need the breaking effect of the rope. Since the snow is so dry I don't tend to gain too much speed when I slide. After retrieving the rope and rolling it up I just sit down and start sliding downhill. This is easy enough to do. The only problem is keeping my slide under control. I need a steering wheel.

In only a few minutes I have descended back down to the point where I had left my pack and sleeping bag. It took almost four hours to go up this distance and had required almost all my strength. Coming down is almost too easy.

I pick up my pack, put it on and start walking downhill. Walking is difficult going down, but does not require nearly the effort climbing up did. I should make the cabin before dark if nothing happens to delay me.

Chapter 22

Our Luck Goes Bad

Just as the sky is starting to grow dark the old cabin comes into view. I never dreamed that such a broken down old cabin could look so wonderful.

It takes me another hour to finally reach the cabin. It is almost totally dark by the time I manage to reach the window. I call out to Ginger and am greatly relieved when she pushes the window open and looks down on me. She looks at me as if she is surprised to see me alive.

"Did you get through to Jack?"

"Yeah, I did. He has the message and, if I know Jack, he is on his way to your father's plane by now."

I look at the window and come to the realization that I will never be able to climb my way up and into it. I turn and start walking toward the front. I will be leaving tracks at the front of the cabin, but this can't be helped. I am so tired and hungry that I have a difficult time coming in the door. Ginger sees how beat I am. She comes over and helps me take off the pack. "How much firewood do we have left Kid?"

"Just about enough to make one good fire is all," she answers.

"Good! Let's build a fire, get warm and then eat a meal"

"What do you want to eat?"

"Anything as long as it isn't beef jerky," I reply.

While Ginger is going through the pack looking for something for dinner I get to work building a fire. I am so cold that my shivering shakes out two matches before Ginger sees my plight and comes to my aid. She lights the fire with her first match and then gives me a look of superiority. I am so grateful for the heat that I don't mind feeling inferior.

After we have eaten we spend some time talking about our experiences while we were apart. Ginger would never admit that she felt fear, but she did say she feels better now that we are together again. I open my sleeping bag and set it near the fire to dry out the dampness caused by the snow on my boots last night. Being so tired added to the full tummy and warm fire makes me so sleepy that I crawl into my sleeping bag while Ginger is still telling me of her adventures during the time I was away.

I wake up to the sound of Ginger tromping around in the cabin. Every inch of my body aches. It is with great effort that I manage to crawl out of my sleeping bag. Ginger looks over at me and raises one finger to her lips. I soon hear why she is doing so. I too hear voices. They do not sound too close to our location, but I fear that may not last much longer.

All of a sudden I forget about all of my body aches. I crawl on all fours over to my bow and quiver of arrows. I grab them and crawl over to the door where Ginger is looking out through one of its many cracks.

"Can you see anybody," I whisper to Ginger?

"Not yet, but their voices sound like they are coming closer. I have been hearing them for some time now. Do you think they are friend or foe?"

"Right now if it isn't Jack, Chuck, or Mary I am going to consider them as foe."

All the while I am whispering this to Ginger I am removing an arrow from my quiver and notching it into the bow.

Ginger looks over and sees what I am doing. She whispers, "I sure wish you had a gun instead of that fool bow and those few arrows"

I nod that I am in full agreement with her. We will need to have a good plan and a whole lot of luck if we are going to survive this. I whisper to Ginger telling her to move the packs and sleeping bags to the front of the cabin where they will be behind the door when it is open. From there they won't be noticeable to anyone coming in until they are fully inside. I stay at the door until I see three men coming into site. I strain to hear as much of what they are saying as possible.

The first guy says, "It looks like those two guys were telling the truth about there being a cabin up here. As drunk as they were I wasn't any too sure they knew what they were talking about."

The second guy looks around and then he says, "There are tracks near the door. Those two hikers didn't make them. They said they left when it started snowing. You go up and check out the cabin. We will wait here to make sure they don't leave by a backdoor or go out a window."

With this the first guy pulls a handgun from beneath his coat and starts toward the cabin. I move back away from the door as far as I can while remaining at the front of the cabin. I am counting on his not being able to see us in the darkness of the cabin after coming in from the brightness of the outdoors. All of that snow makes it pretty bright out there.

I haven't much more that gotten myself into position when I hear the fellow step up on the porch. He kicks the door open while remaining on the porch. This doesn't fit my plan too well, but I will just have to make do with whatever he does. After all I can't give him a script of how I want him to play his part.

The guy which appears to be in charge yells up to the fellow on the porch and asks. "Is there anybody inside Claude?"

"I don't see anybody, but it is pretty dark in there I think I will go on in and check it out Pete."

With this statement he steps through the door and takes a couple of steps. I release my arrow and down the fellow goes. His gun flies half way across the cabin and lands about fifteen feet from me. I lurch forward and grab the gun. The fellow never made a noise except for the thud of his body hitting the floor. I hear one of the fellows outside calling out.

"Hey Claude what's going on in there? Did you fall down or something?"

After not hearing a response from his cohort he says, "Quit clowning around in there Claude."

After he again gets no response I hear footsteps in the snow coming towards the cabin. I raise the automatic pistol and point it at the door opening. I have it aimed about chest height for a normal sized man. I hear him step up on the creaky old porch and then stop. I am not sure if he can see his cohort on the floor or not. Suddenly he yells an oath and starts spraying bullets all around the cabin. I have the advantage over him in as much as I know where he is and he has no idea where we are. His shots are all going toward the back of the cabin, but I can't count on him to continue shooting where Ginger and I aren't. I dive over toward the door and fire several shots through it even before I land. The fellow goes down and he shoots no more. I stand up and look out the door to see what the third fellow is doing. He is running downhill faster than I would have thought possible on these snowy trails.

Ginger runs over to me and throws her arms around me. As the adrenaline rush starts to subside I realize what the kid has just seen. I figure she must be in a total state of shock so I drop the pistol and pull her tight to me. I am not sure what good a hug can do at a time like this, but I must say it is reassuring to me. Just as I am trying to think of something to say that might help Ginger cope with the horror she has just witnessed she speaks, "Good job, Old Man. I never thought you had it in you to put up such a good fight. Do you think it is safe to leave here now? Do you think it is safe to go back to your cabin now? I'll bet that other guy doesn't stop running for a week. You sure put the fear in him."

So much for worrying about the Kid being traumatized by what she has seen, or maybe this is her way of coping with the trauma she has just been through. I am finally able to loosen my tongue enough to speak. "I don't know the answer to all of your questions Kid, but I think I had better check these two guys out. They could still be alive."

I release my arms from around Ginger and stand up. I walk over to the fellow lying on the floor. He is still breathing. My arrow went through his neck, but he is not bleeding very much. It must not have hit the jugular or carotid. He appears to be unconscious, but this could just be an act so I will keep an eye on him while I check out the fellow on the porch.

As I reach him and bend down I find he is still breathing too. The only wound I find on him is a graze wound on the forehead. He must be unconscious also. I don't think he is badly hurt, but I don't envy him the headache he will have when he comes around. I yell for Ginger to bring me the rope. When she arrives with it I put the pistol in my pocket and then tie the fellow's hands and feet with the rope. This should hold him if he comes around. I start looking around for the gun he was holding, when I shot him. After considerable looking I find it in a snow drift against the cabin. I then empty his pockets. I find extra clips, for this pistol, money and a car key, nothing else. With this fellow taken care of I go back inside the cabin and secure the hands and feet of the other fellow. I am glad that I have killed no one, but now what do I do with two wounded criminals on the side of a snowy mountain? I guess these same thoughts must be running through Ginger's head because she asks, "What are we going to do with these two guys?" Then almost as if she is answering her own question she says, "Maybe we should just leave them and get out of here."

"No Kid, as despicable as these guys may be I can't do that. If we did that we would be no better than they are."

While I am talking to Ginger I go through the other fellow's pockets. Again, I find extra clips for his pistol, money and nothing else. At least they are consistent.

I go outside and drag the fellow on the porch inside and lay him next to the other fellow. He is a heavy weight. I would judge that he must outweigh me by a good deal even though he is not near as tall as me. I look over to Ginger and say, "I suggest we wrap up in our sleeping bags to keep warm. We will wait for a while to see if either of these sleeping beauties wake up. After we find out just how badly hurt they are we will have a better idea what our options are."

Ginger climbs in her sleeping bag in the sitting position. I open up the pack containing what little food we have remaining. I select some kippered herring and crackers. Not a great meal, but maybe after eating this we will be able to control these two criminal types with our breath, if they wake up that is. I pull my sleeping bag over next to Ginger and climb in it in the sitting position also. We share the herring and crackers in silence. After a few bites it becomes apparent that I have forgotten something. I climb out of the sleeping bag and go back to the pack and get a couple of bottles of water. As I am handing Ginger one of the bottles I hear a moan. Glancing over at our guests I notice the fellow with the arrow throw his throat is struggling to get himself to the sitting position. I set down the bottle of water I have in my hand and walk over and assist him to the sitting position. I notice a large bump on his forehead. That must be what rendered him unconscious.

"Can you talk," I ask? He makes no attempt to respond to my question. I try no more to get him to communicate. He doesn't appear to be too much of a threat to us now so I return to my sleeping bag and my breakfast.

Some time after we finish our breakfast I notice the second fellow is moving his body as if he wants to sit up. I walk over and help him into an upright position also. Maybe this fellow will be a little more willing to communicate than his partner has been. "Can you talk," I ask?

"Yeah, I can talk," he says followed by an oath such that an old seadog would envy.

"Okay mister, we may not like each other too much, but I think we are kind of in the same fix here and if we want to live we will need to work together. Do you think you can walk if I untie you feet?"

"Yeah, I think I can," he responds.

I bend down and start untying the rope binding his feet. When they are free he draws them up toward his body. I think nothing of this move. I figure he is trying to restore circulation in his legs. As I am picking up the rope to put it back in the pack I hear Ginger yell, "look out John!"

At about the same time I feel a great weight hit me and a horrendous pain in my left shoulder. This felon has jumped me! With all the power I can muster up I heave myself into a standing position. The fat little hood rolls off my back and lands on the floor with a huge thud. I reach back to see what is causing the pain in my shoulder. I find the handle of a small knife. He must have had a boot knife and I was dumb enough not only to fail to find it, but to allow him the opportunity to use it. By now I have drawn the pistol from my coat pocket and have it pushed up to his forehead right between his eyes. "You idiot," I say! "Now there are four of us up here snowed in with little food, little water and no wood for heat. Thanks to you, three of us are wounded and the other weighs less than 80 pounds. You have just about ended our possibility of getting out of here alive." I am so mad that I have to keep reminding myself what I told Ginger regarding what sets us apart from them.

The fat little punk doesn't look like he is in the mood for continuing the fight. I pull the pistol out of this his face and put it back in my pocket. Then in a measured voice I tell him, "We are going to walk out of here and back to my cabin. You will assist your buddy and since you have wounded me you will also carry my pack and sleeping bag. It is my full intention for all of us to get to my cabin safely, but if only two of us can make it then Ginger and I will be the ones who do. Is that understood?"

"Yeah, I get it."

With this I slowly move across the floor to where Ginger is. She looks up and says, "Do you want me to pull the knife out of your back?"

"No Kid. I fear removing the knife from my back or the arrow from that fellow's neck could cause bleeding so we will just leave them where they are at least until we get back to my cabin."

Ginger appears relieved that she need not remove the knife.

While I am keeping my eye on the two criminals Ginger closes the packs, rolls the sleeping bags and attaches them to the packs. I walk over to the fellow with my arrow in his neck and ask him, "Do you think you can walk if I untie your feet?"

He nods in the affirmative. Ginger has already put her pack on. I motion for Fat Boy to go over and put on the other one, which he does moving about as slow as molasses would pour in this weather. I tell him, "Go untie your buddy and help him up. You two take the lead. That way, if we are ambushed, the two of you will make a good shield for Ginger and me."

Fat Boy goes over unties his buddy's feet, helps him up and they head for the door with Ginger and I close behind. Walking is slow and difficult. We have to veer off the trail often to avoid the snow which has drifted over the trail. I am trying to keep my left arm immobile to prevent the knife from doing any further damage to the flesh around it. I am surprised how well the fellow with my arrow in his neck is doing. He is keeping up with his buddy seemingly without too much difficulty. We must reach my cabin by nightfall or the two hoods will suffer hyperthermia and frostbite since they have no sleeping bags.

No one has said anything since we left the old cabin. I guess the conditions we are facing are not conducive to conversation. We all just keep walking, lost in our own thoughts. My thoughts are mostly of the weather. It is growing dark way too early. My guess is we are in for a snow and most likely it will not be too long in coming. This is not a pleasant thought since we still are not quite half way back to my cabin. I try hard to avoid thinking about how weak I am starting to feel. If I conclude that I am going to pass out or maybe die, I feel I will have no choice but to kill the two would-be assassins before I do. If I don't, heaven knows what they might do to Ginger. Thinking about the possibilities of what might happen if I can't keep on going helps me to find the courage to keep putting one foot in front of the other.

When we finally reach an area that looks familiar to me I realize we are only a few hundred yards from my cabin. I guess the snow has made things look so different that it took me quite some time to recognize the features I should know really well.

I am amazed that we have made it to here considering three of us are wounded and Ginger is so small that even walking behind three of us, making a trail for her has to be very difficult.

My cabin is in sight and a beautiful site it is. We continue walking, stumbling, getting up and walking some more until we are on the back porch and then on inside. I invite our guests to sit in the two best chairs in my living room. Of course I do this because the chairs have arms and will be easy to use to immobilize them. After they are seated I have Ginger get the duct tape and tape their arms and legs to the chairs. With this accomplished I start a fire in the fireplace. The effort required to do this has taken most of the strength left in me.

CHAPTER 23

GINGER TAKES CHARGE

I walk over to the table and sit down on one of the chairs. I don't recall ever feeling this weak. I motion for Ginger to join me. When she sits down in the chair closest to mine I say in as low a voice as I can and still have Ginger understand me, "Ginger since we met I have tried every way I can to protect you. Now I fear I need you to take charge. I am so weak that I don't think I can do anything further, yet we need to eat and these fellows need to be watched. If you will, go to the pantry and get a couple of cans of potato soup and heat them. Do you know how to use the stove?"

"Yes, I watched you and it didn't look too complicated to me."

"Okay, do that and when the soup is hot pour it into four bowls."

Before I can say anything more Ginger pipes up saying, "Four bowls? You aren't going to feed those idiots are you?"

"Yes Ginger, we are. Remember if we don't we are lowering ourselves to their level and we don't want to do that do we?"

Ginger just nods and then goes into the kitchen and starts preparing our dinner. I try to keep a watch on our guests but I keep nodding off to sleep. It can't be the wound that has me so beaten. I don't seem to have lost too much blood and the pain isn't all that bad as long as I keep my left arm immobile. It must be the combination of all the effort required to climb the mountain coupled with the extreme cold. I can't ever remember shivering as much in my entire life as I did during that climb.

Ginger brings me a bowl of soup and spoon. It tastes a little scorched, but it is still delicious after a diet of beef jerky and tinned meat. I watch as Ginger feeds the fat fellow. He eats greedily and behaves himself until Ginger has fed him all that was in his bowl. He asks for more but Ginger just goes over to the other fellow and tries to get him to eat. He just shakes his head and looks away. I fear his wound won't allow him to eat. I almost feel sorry for him. I would never have chosen to shoot him there but I was just aiming to bring him down not for a specific spot. It is not a very comforting feeling to know that my marksmanship is so poor. I squeezed off five shots at Fat Boy and only managed to produce an almost superficial wound on his forehead. Oh well, it all turned out in our favor. At least so far it has.

Ginger brings her bowl of soup over to the table and sits down beside me. I have almost finished eating my soup when she comes over. I must admit the soup has increased my strength, but has added to my sleepiness as well. I wait until Ginger has finished her bowl of soup and then I whisper to her. "Ginger, I am so sleepy I will never be able to stay awake to watch these guys. Do you think you can watch them?"

"Sure thing, John."

"Okay. I am going to give you one of the pistols and show you how to use it. I am doing this mostly to keep these guys thinking they are being guarded but if anything starts to go wrong just wake me and I will handle it. Use the pistol only if you can't get a response from me and the situation is dire. Do you understand?"

"Yes, I understand. You just get some sleep and don't worry about me. Okay?"

I hand one of the pistols to Ginger and show her how to release the safety and to pull the trigger. "If you start to feel sleepy, wake me up and I will take over for a while." With this I get to my feet, walk over to the lower bunk and lay face down on it.

I wake up to the sound of fat boy's whiny voice saying, "For Pete's sake Kid cut me loose. I've got to go."

Ginger responds with, "Hey, you came here to kill me, so you can just sit there and pee your pants. I'm not about to cut you loose so you can finish what you came here to do."

I stand up and walk over to the chair fat boy is taped to and pull out my knife. I cut the tape holding his left hand and then tell him, "go ahead and free yourself, but bear in mind that if you act like you are going to do anything but go to the bathroom the Kid is going to shoot you."

I must have slept all night because it is full light outside and it is snowing hard. So hard in fact that I can hardly see to the nearest tree. On the positive side we are still alive and have control of our pursuers. On the negative side we are snowed in and a good part of the gas for the generator is up at the old cabin where we left it. We have four mouths to feed, which will deplete our food supply in a few days. Our supply of firewood will also be depleted in a couple of days if we can't get to the pile behind the generator shed. Finally, three of us are wounded and in need of medical care. All-in-all I would say the negatives outweigh the positives. This seems to be a trend since Ginger and I met.

About this time fat boy comes out of the bathroom. He is as pale as a ghost. He takes about two steps and falls flat on his face. I approach him cautiously not sure if he has really passed out or if this is a ploy trying to gain control over me.

When I bend down to check him out it becomes evident that this is not an act. He appears to be in a bad way. I cannot get him back into the chair because my own wound prohibits me from using my left arm. My only option for now is to tape his wrists and ankles. We will try to keep him as warm and comfortable as possible. Ginger sees my plight and comes to my aid. She brings a blanket and throws it over fat boy. I take a cushion from one of the chairs and put it under his head. Ginger says nothing but I get the idea she doesn't approve of my coddling this guy. I imagine I will hear about this later.

Ginger walks about half-way across the floor then turns and says, "What are we going to do now? We can't just wait around here with a knife sticking out of your shoulder, an arrow sticking out of that guy's neck to say nothing about that guy laying there unconscious can we?"

"You're right about that Kid. It appears the weather and our physical conditions are going to prevent us from getting out of here so I guess we will need to do what we can for ourselves until we do get out of here."

"Surely you have some method of getting out of here in the winter don't you Old Man?"

"Normally during the winter I park my car at the bottom of the driveway and use my snowmobile to get to it and back to the cabin but we were not here to move my car so it is still in the garage."

"So what you are saying is we are in a total mess. Do you think it would do any good to complain to God?"

"I'm not sure Kid, but I think God hears a lot more complaints than he does thanks. It appears that we just need to be thankful for the things we have going for us."

"Things we have going for us? Pray tell me what we have going for us right now?"

"Well, let me see. We are alive, we are inside and sheltered from the storm, we are in charge of our pursuers, we have food, water and firewood enough for a few more days and the storm that is keeping us here is preventing other pursuers from coming after us. I think I am going to thank the Lord for these things."

Ginger looks at me like I am some kind of a nut. Who knows she may be right. Then she says, "What is it with that Fat Boy anyway? Is he just pretending? He didn't appear to be in too bad a condition when he stabbed you. After all, he just got grazed across the forehead. I wouldn't think that would be too serious a wound."

"I am not sure Kid, but I fear he may be worse off than any of us. That bullet that grazed his forehead was equal to a glancing blow from a sledgehammer. He may have a concussion or he may have bone splinters inside his scull. He also took a nasty bump on the back of his head when he fell, after I shot him.

Do you think you can pull the Knife out of my shoulder? There is no way I can reach it well enough to pull it out without doing further damage to myself."

"Sure I can. Just tell me what to do and I will do it."

"Okay, go into the bathroom and get a hand towel."

Ginger immediately takes off for the bathroom and in a few seconds she is back with a hand towel.

"Now what do you want me to do?"

"Okay. Fold the towel several times. When you have this done place it just below the knife and pull the knife out of my shoulder. Don't pay any attention to my reactions just pull it out as straight as you can. When the knife is out, quickly put the towel over the wound."

I have hardly finished saying the last word when I feel the towel press up against my shoulder and then feel the knife being pulled out. Surprisingly I don't feel a great deal of pain. Ginger throws the knife on the table and says, "What now Old Man?"

"Remove the towel and see how badly it bleeds. If there is a great deal of bleeding put the towel back on the wound and hold it there as tightly as you can. If there is not much bleeding just leave the towel off and help me get my coat and shirt off."

I feel Ginger remove the towel but she says nothing for a few moments. When she speaks it is to say, "I don't see any bleeding at all."

I am surprised to hear this. I expected at least some bleeding. Maybe my shirt and undershirt are absorbing the blood. While thinking this and with Ginger's help, I remove my coat, shirt and undershirt. When I pull off the undershirt Ginger says, "It's bleeding now. What should I do?"

"Look in the pack I usually carry. There is a first aid kit in it. Bring it here and we will fashion a bandage for my wound."

Ginger does as instructed and between us we managed to make and put on a suitable bandage saturated with antibiotic ointment. Now that I am attended to we need to turn our attention to our wounded guests.

I walk over to the fellow with the arrow through his neck. His head is laying back and his eyes are closed. I would think he was dead if I didn't see he is breathing. I ask if he is doing okay. His eyes open and he nods his head indicating he is. I then start to give it to him as straight as I can. "Listen mister, I wouldn't have chosen to shoot you in the neck. It just happens that is where my arrow went. I don't know much beyond some basic first aid, but I don't think it is good to leave that arrow in your neck. If you move and hit it on something it could do you more damage. Would you like for me to remove it?"

He nods his head in the affirmative.

"Okay, I will have to remove the tip from the arrow to reduce the likelihood of doing further damage to tissue when I remove the arrow. There are major arteries and veins in your neck. If I nick one of those there won't be much I can do for you. You are aware of this aren't you?"

Again he nods his head indicating he understands. I walk over to my toolbox and remove my battery operated, rotary cutting tool. I am about to do surgery using tools designed for doing wood work. I look over at Ginger. She doesn't appear to be too grossed out by what I am doing so I say, "how about giving me a hand over here Kid?"

"What are you thinking? Are you going to help this guy? He tried to kill us, you know."

"Yes, Kid I do know, but the Bible says to be kind to your enemies so I am going to do as it says and give this guy aid."

"Sometimes I wonder about your Bible. It doesn't make sense to me to give help to someone who got his wound trying to kill us. I hope you don't help him enough for him to feel up to trying to kill us all over again."

"I don't think you have to worry about that Kid. I just hope we can avoid his dying on us. No more than I know about medicine he might be better off if I was to do nothing, but we will give this our best try anyway."

"What do you mean 'we', Old Man?"

"Just what I said Kid. Now come over here and hold this guy's head still while I remove the tip from this arrow."

A tortoise with lumbago could have moved faster than Ginger does coming to my aid. At least she is coming. I only hope she is coming to help and not looking for revenge. When she finally arrives she asks, "What do you want me to do?"

"Just hold his head and try to keep him from moving it while I am cutting the tip off of the arrow. Okay?"

"Okay I have it," Ginger says as she puts one hand on either side of the Claude's head.

I mutter a quick prayer asking the Lord for a steady hand and the guts to go through with this. I then take a grip on the arrow on the side protruding from his neck in the best way my injured left arm will allow and start to cut through the arrow shaft with my rotary cutter. To my surprise my patient sits perfectly still throughout the process of cutting the arrow shaft. Once this process is complete I clean the arrow with rubbing alcohol. I lubricate the arrow shaft with mineral oil to reduce the friction during the removal process. I have no idea if this is a good thing to do or not, but it seems logical to me.

I look at Claude only to see he has his eyes shut and his teeth clinched tight. "Okay mister I am going to remove the arrow now. If you can keep from moving your head the likelihood of your surviving this procedure will be greatly enhanced. Do you think you can do this?"

He blinks his eyes which I take as an affirmative answer so I proceed with the removal of the arrow. I am greatly relieved when there is no spurt or spew of blood. I make up two bandages and dab a liberal amount of antibiotic ointment on each of them before taping them to the wounds on each side of the Claude's neck.

"Okay Ginger you can release your grip on the guy's head."

When she removes her hands our patient lays his head back on the chair back never opening his eyes, but I do believe he is no longer clinching his teeth.

I am hungry and it is nearly lunch time. We never had breakfast this morning. I walk into the kitchen and grab a can of soup to heat. Ginger follows me in and it is a good thing she does. I find that a manual can opener is a difficult tool to use with only one arm in good operating condition.

I can tell by the look on Ginger's face that she is about to hit me with one of her weighty questions. I am not disappointed. She looks up to me and says, "It seems to me that this God you worship isn't too practical a fellow. He tells you to do good for your enemies. Surely he realizes that they have tried to harm you in the past and are likely to do so again in the future, if given the opportunity.

"I know Kid. It is difficult to understand love so strong that it will forgive you regardless of what you have done, but it does exist. In the prayer His son Jesus taught us to pray, "Forgive us our sins as we forgive those who have sinned against us". This kind of puts the ball in our hands. If we want to be forgiven of our sins we need to forgive those who have sinned against us. God wants us to have unconditional love for others like he has for us."

"And you do this? Ginger says with a note of curiosity in her voice"

"I fear I fail at it a lot, but I keep trying. I hope you will too"

With this said we continue with our preparations for lunch. It only takes a few minutes of my fumbling everything I touch, trying to work with only one fully operational arm, before Ginger decides that I am completely useless and takes over the cooking duties. Left with nothing else to do I walk over and check on our guests. The fellow we removed the arrow from appears to be sleeping. His breathing is regular and not labored. I can't say as much for the fellow on the floor. His breathing is labored and his color is pale. I feel of his chest. His heart is beating as fast as if he had just completed running a marathon. About this time I see Ginger carrying our soup to the table. I walk over and join her. She is sitting waiting for me to say grace. At least she has gotten used to the idea of our saying grace before we eat.

After I say grace, Ginger starts eating her soup. I wait a couple of minutes before broaching the subject I have on my mind. I try to organize my thoughts so they will make sense to the Kid, but I soon surrender. I'm not even sure they make sense to me. I'll just say what I intend to do. "Ginger, in the morning I am going to get the snowmobile out of the garage and see if I can get it started. I need to get help up here or I fear that the hood on the floor may not make it."

Ginger looks up at me like I must be totally out of my mind. Then she lights into me like a cat attacking its prey. "What do you care? This guy has tried time and again to kill us and now you are worried that he may die? What's the matter with you anyway Old Man? Are you crazy or something? You know if he gets better he will try to kill us again don't you? Besides, if you get help up here for him they will take us back to town again and this time they will throw you in jail and I'll be taken to some kind of a foster home or something. If they do that how are we going to protect each other?"

I guess she finally ran out of breath because she hesitated just long enough that I can butt in to explain myself. "I am going to help these fellows out because that is what God would have me to do. He cares for all of us regardless of whether we are good or not. I guess He feels it is important that these guys live so they have time to mend their ways and repent."

Ginger looks at me with a look of total disgust on her face. Then she says, "This God of yours is going to get us killed, you know."

I say nothing and start eating my soup. It tastes burnt. I don't think the Kid will ever learn to cook and I doubt she will ever understand me either.

After dinner I get up and start out the back door.

"Where are you going, Ginger asks?"

"I'm going out to the generator shed and start up the generator. When that is done I am going to change the tank for the gas heater. I would hate for the plumbing to freeze up while we are away."

"Gas heater, I didn't know you had a gas heater in here? It's always cold as an ice cube when you don't have a fire in the fireplace," Ginger says with a note of surprise in her voice.

"I know the heater is set to come on only if the temperature drops below forty degrees in here. It is only protection against the plumbing freezing"

"Well turn it up so we don't keep freezing our butts every morning."

"I'm sorry Kid I can't do that. It burns the gas too quickly if I turn it up very high and I only have one spare tank left after I make this change."

With the explanations completed, I walk on out the back door and over to the generator shed. Gassing up the generator is a rough chore with only one arm, but it is a piece of cake compared to changing out the tank for the heater.

When I come back into the cabin, I am surprised to note that Ginger has cleaned up the dishes from dinner. I walk over to the fellow bound in the chair and ask him if he would like to go to the bathroom. He nodded that he would so I cut the tape loose from his arms and legs. He totters off to the bathroom. After a few minutes he returns and sits back in the chair and assumes the position for me to tape his arms and legs again. I look at him. It is apparent that he is getting very weak.

"I don't know much about medicine, but I know enough to realize that you are going to become dehydrated if you don't drink something. Do you think you can swallow some water if I get you some?"

He nods his head in the affirmative. So I go into the kitchen and get a small glass of water and take it to him. Before I hand it to him I say, "I do know enough to realize that an object can't penetrate the neck without hitting some vital areas. I have no idea what is damaged in there so I suggest you try a small sip and then wait a while to see what happens before drinking more. Okay Claude?"

"Okay John," he says in a very low, raspy voice.

To my surprise he seems to tolerate the water very well. I leave it with him and go back over to set up the batteries on their charges. Ginger is keeping a wary eye on Claude. I don't think she much approves of my allowing him to remain unsecured to the chair.

After a couple of hours I walk over and tape Claude's arms and legs back to the chair. Then I go out and shut down the generator. When I come back in the only light in the cabin is the eerie dancing light given off by the fireplace. Ginger has added enough wood to it that we now have a raging fire going.

We don't even light a lantern. Ginger is already in her bunk and it is not long before I crawl into my bunk. Sleep comes quickly.

Chapter 24

Jack and More Criminals Show Up

I wake with a start. Something or someone has made a noise. I lay perfectly still waiting to see if I hear anything else. After a few minutes I hear the noise again. It is Pete. He is conscious again and he doesn't seem to be in too good of a mood judging from the oath he just swore. I will worry about him later. Right now I am more concerned about how cold I am. Ginger is right about the temperature being frigid after the fire has been out for a while. I am shivering with the covers over me. What will it be like when I throw them back and get out of bed? I muster up enough courage to throw the covers back. By the time I have my robe and house shoes on, my teeth are chattering like a chipmunk.

It appears the snow is over. It is very discouraging to look outside. The snow is deep. I would guess it is close to three feet deep. Oh well, there is not much I can do about this so I guess I may as well get the fire started.

I remove the ashes from last night's fire and then reach over to get some wood to start the fire. There may be enough wood left inside for today, but we will need to get some wood from the pile outside before tomorrow.

Finally, I have a roaring fire going, but I still can't seem to stop shivering. My head hurts and my shoulder is killing me. All of this doesn't have me in the mood to put up with Pete's bellyaching. I walk over and ask him what his problem is.

"I'm cold and I have to go p—-," he says in his normal eloquent manner.

I reach down and pull the cover off of him then I cut the tape from his hands. I am fascinated by his seemingly quick recovery. Last night I thought he was near death and now, just a few hours later, he is back to his old, obnoxious self.

After noting the look on his face while he is removing the tape from his ankles, I pull the pistol from my pocket and hold it in my hand just as a reminder to him that he should not try anything stupid. He seems to get the message and heads straight for the bathroom. I walk over to check on Claude. He is awake and in a low and very raspy voice say, "I need to go the bathroom too."

"Okay, as soon as Pete gets back and I have him taped down again."

I have hardly completed saying this when Pete opens the bathroom door and comes out. He again doesn't look too good. I motion for him to come back and be seated in the chair. He makes it but by the time he does he just falls into it. I don't think being upright agrees with his condition. I tape his arms and feet to the chair. I cut Claude's left hand loose and allow him to free his right hand and his feet. When he has done so, he heads for the bathroom.

"Hey, what's for breakfast?" Ginger asks sounding rather impatient. I'm starving. Our diet of soup, jerky and that stinky fish stuff isn't sufficient to keep my tummy satisfied, you know."

"And a good morning to you too. Why don't you hop up and give me a hand and we'll fix a breakfast that will fill that little tummy of yours?"

Ginger gets up, steps into her house shoes and pulls on her robe. By then I have gotten eggs, bacon and frozen home fries out of the refrigerator. I boil the eggs while frying the bacon and heating the fries. Ginger busies herself setting the table. I am not doing too bad cooking with only one hand until it come to using the can opener. At this I need help. Ginger comes to my rescue and opens the can of celery soup I have gotten out for Claude. When it is warm I pour it though a strainer into a glass. Ginger helps me as we peel the eggs and make up three plates of food. Ginger takes mine and hers to the table while I take a plate to Pete and the glass of soup to Claude. I cut the tape holding Pete and Claude's left arms and allow them to feed themselves. Then I join Ginger at the table for breakfast.

"What's with you Old Man? You are shaking all over. Are you cold or something?"

"I don't know. I just can't seem to get warm this morning. After I eat I'll get dressed and maybe I will get warm then."

Ginger and I finish eating in silence. Claude appears to be doing all right with his strained soup, but Pete has hardly eaten anything. I walk over and tape our guest's arms again. Then I get dressed.

Ginger walks over to where I am standing and says, "Are we getting out of here today?"

"That's my plan if all works out."

"That snow is awful deep out there. Do you think you can walk through it?"

"No. I plan to walk on top of it."

"What are you telling me, are you a magician or something?"

"Not quite, but I do have snowshoes"

I walk over and take them from the wall where they hang and start to strap them on. After I have finally managed to get them on I put on my heavy coat, pull my hat on with, ear flaps down, and put on my mittens. Now I have gone from cold and shivering to burning hot. Maybe when I get outside I will be comfortable.

"Okay Kid, here is one of the pistols. You keep an eye on these two until I get back with the snowmobile. Okay?"

"Okay, but don't take too long. I'm awful tempted to shoot that fat guy, you know." she says with a sly grin on her face.

I know she said this for his benefit, but from his appearance I don't think he is in any condition to give her much trouble. I go out to the generator shed and grab a couple of gallons of gas, then head around the cabin and start toward the garage. Before I make it more that a couple of dozen steps I hear the sound of a snowmobile. It sounds like it is coming our way.

I head for the nearest big tree and step behind it while pulling my right mitten off using my teeth. Once it is removed I put my hand in my coat pocket and grip the pistol I am carrying. About this time the snowmobile comes into sight. I wait until it pulls up in front of the cabin and the rider steps off then I pull the pistol out of my pocket and say, "Hold it right there mister and keep your hands in plain sight or I'll have to shoot."

"Hey, John, don't shoot. It's me Jack."

"What are you doing out here. Don't you know the weather isn't fit for man or beast?"

"No. Nobody told me until you just did."

"Well let's get into the cabin. There is no sense staying out here in the cold."

"Well, I'm not about to argue with you regarding that."

Ginger has the cabin door open just a crack and I can see the nose of her pistol sticking through the crack.

"Hey Jack, maybe you should let Ginger have a good look at you before she shoots."

Jack looks toward the cabin and when he sees the pistol pointed his way he takes his hat off and yells "Don't shoot me Ginger. It's Jack. John and I are coming in."

Ginger flings the door open and yells, "Come on in. I won't shoot."

Jack grabs a bundle off of the mobile and heads into the cabin. It takes me a little longer to get there.

When we are both in the cabin and have our coats, hats and mittens off I can retain my curiosity no longer. "Did you get into the locker in the Memphis bus station?"

"Well, I found the key. You were right it was hidden in Carlo's plane, but when I got to the Memphis bus station I found there was no locker one-one-three. There is a locker two-one-three, but the key isn't even the right type of key for the lock. I had no idea where I should go from there so I came back. Chuck, Mary and I have been putting our heads together trying to come up with what we should do next, but so far we haven't come up with much of an idea. By the way, why are we whispering?"

I nod toward the chairs Claude and Pete are taped to and say, "We have guests. I don't intend for them to get away, but I don't think it would be good to have them know too much."

"Oh. I see what you mean."

"I'm not sure but I think I have learned a little about how Carlos thinks. I don't think the final code of his message was a direction to a location like we thought it was but, rather, is another clue. It most likely has to do with Memphis, greyhound terminal, and the combination of the numbers one-one-three. We just need to put that part of the puzzle together and we will have the information we need to find what he left us."

"Okay John. I'll give you that much, but do you have any idea how to put this all together."

"I'm sorry to say it Jack, but I haven't the foggiest idea. I think one of us will need to make a trip to Memphis and see if we can figure out the location by following the clues."

"Okay John, maybe you should be the one to go. You figured out his code. How did you do that anyway?"

"Well, it helped that Ginger gave me the clue her mother had told her. Without that I might still be working on deciphering Carlo's code."

Jack looks over at Ginger and asks, "Did your mother give you any other clues Kid?"

"No, that was the only one and my Dad never gave me any either."

"Are you sure Kid? Maybe you just don't remember."

I can see Ginger's face getting red. I think she has had about all she can take of being called Kid. That seems to be a right she reserves only for me. She also doesn't take too well to being suspected of not remembering anything. I feel it is about time I step in between Jack and Ginger before a full fledged war breaks out.

"Jack, one thing I have learned is if Ginger hears something she won't forget it. If she says there were no other clues given to her then you can bet there were no other clues given to her.'

Jack looks at me and then says, "Could the clue she gave you help in solving this mystery as well?"

"Now that's something I never thought about, Jack. It might apply here too."

"What was the clue? Maybe, if we all know the riddle and the clue, one of us might come up with the answer."

"As best I remember it I think it went something like this 'the first is to be expected, the second is simple, and the third repeats itself'."

Jack, with a puzzled look on his face, says, "Is that it? Is that all there is to the hint?"

"I'm afraid that's all there is, but it was enough to help solve his code." By the way my curiosity is getting the better of me. What do you have in the bag you brought with you?"

"Oh, there are a couple of rifles and a few boxes of ammunition in there. Chuck insisted that I give them to you if I were to see you. He said to tell you that he thinks you need a little better arsenal than just your bow and a few arrows. He thinks you are up against some kind of professionals. He also said to tell you that he hasn't convinced any of the other law enforcement agencies of this though. They still tend to think this is just a local problem. They feel the investigations they made after Carlo's death showed nothing to support any conspiracy theory"

Ginger breaks up the chummy little conversation Jack and I are having by saying, "I hear snowmobiles. Was anyone else with you Jack?"

"No, I came alone."

"Maybe it is time for us to get the rifles out of that bag and load them just in case whoever's coming isn't friendly, I say while pulling the pistol out of my coat pocket along with the spare clips."

"Yeah, John that sounds like a good idea to me."

Jack begins pulling the rifles and boxes of ammunition from the bag. He throws one of the rifles to me. I catch it with my right hand and then hand it back to him. "I'm afraid I won't be able to use this Pete planted a knife in my shoulder and my left arm is pretty useless now."

I motion for Ginger to move away from behind the door and get behind the thick log wall. Jack is busy loading both rifles. I move over to the wall adjacent to the door so I can look though the door, which is still open just a crack. I do this while keeping the log wall between me and any projectile that might come flying our way.

In a couple of minutes four snowmobiles roar up the path from my driveway. Three of them stop in front of the cabin but one continued on around to the back. Just that quick all of our avenues of escape are cut off.

When the men dismounted their machines, it quickly becomes evident that they have come prepared to do battle. They all carry semi-automatic weapons. Most likely they have been modified to fire fully automatic. This is not a comforting thought. Jack moves over to where I am, dragging the two rifles with him.

"Okay John, do you have a plan or are we just going to make it up as we go?"

"We will use the advantages we have available to us"

Before I can say anymore Jack says, "Advantages? Tell me what advantages we have. All I can see right now are disadvantages,"

"Don't be so negative Jack. The kid and I have been through this twice before and came out on top. Admittedly, the fellows didn't have automatic rifles before, but I think the same tactics that worked then will work again. First, let's get up in the loft and I will explain my plan to you there."

"Okay," Jack says, already on the move toward the steps.

I motion for Ginger to follow him and then I bring up the rear. Once we are in the loft I take a quick look out the observation ports to make sure our guests are still in sight. As I feared only two are still in sight in the front of the cabin. This must mean that one of them has moved in close to the cabin where I can no longer keep watch on him. I move as close to the front wall of the cabin as I can and then motion for Jack and Ginger to do likewise.

Jack says, "Tell me your plan John."

"There is no time for that now. Just join in the fight when it starts. Right now I need to listen for anyone coming up on the porch. Okay?"

"Okay."

All remains silent for a few minutes, then a burst of gun fire comes flying through one of the front windows. The shutters did little to prevent the projectiles from coming through. Then all is silent again for a few minutes. Then I hear footsteps on the porch. The door flings open and bullets come flying. They sweep from one side of the cabin to the other. I fear that Pete and Claude are no longer with us.

After a few seconds the gunman comes flying through the door diving and rolling across the floor. Jack and I open fire and one of us hits him. His rifle is still in his outstretched hand, but he makes no further moves. I quickly take a look through the observation ports. In the front, both of the fellows are visible. In the back the one fellow is still sitting on his snowmobile. I motion for Jack to join me. When he reaches my location I have him take a look through the observation port to the front then I ask him, "Do you think you can hit these guys though the observation port."

"Sure John. Do you want me to shoot through the glass?"

"No give me a minute and I will remove the glass. This will allow you to stick the rifle out the port and rest it on the ledge for a better shot."

As I start removing the glass I feel so light headed. I am not sure I am going to be able to get it ou, ou,ou out.

Chapter 25

Things begin to Fit Together

I slowly start to become aware of my surroundings. I am in a bed, I have a horrible headache and, from the smell, I would guess I am in a hospital. Funny thing is, I have no idea how I got here or why I'm alone. I look for the nurse call button but when I move, I feel like a part of me is going to break off so I give up trying.

I am vaguely aware of someone in the room with me, but it is too dark to see them and just too much effort to say anything. I must have fallen asleep because this time when I open my eyes the room is well lit and I see Chuck standing next to my bed.

"So you finally decided to wake up. Jack said to tell you he's going to quit helping you in your gun battles if you are going to keep taking a nap in the middle them."

I try to answer Chuck but a weak smile is all I can muster up. Chuck keeps on talking. He says, "Jack and Mary have been working on Carlo's instructions. After several hours on the net Mary seemed to have a pretty good hunch of what Carlo's instructions might be saying. She and Jack flew to Memphis to see if they have the location figured out.

I finally muster up the strength to ask the only questions that seems relevant to me. "Where is Ginger? Is she all right?"

Chuck hesitates before saying, "Well that Ms. Blanchard took her as soon as we got all of you back to town. She is not too happy about her being with you. In fact that is pretty much of an understatement. She has scheduled a hearing before Judge Mathis next week to have you declared unfit to be a foster parent. She is also planning to press charges against you for kidnapping Ginger."

I guess all of this should concern me, but my biggest concern is how Ginger is doing and I don't even need to ask. If she is being made to do something she doesn't want to do, I know exactly how she is doing. Not well. Finally, I find enough interest to ask, "Do I need a lawyer?"

"No, I don't think so Ja. I know Judge Mathis well enough to be relatively sure reason will prevail, After all, this is just a hearing."

About this time the doctor comes strolling into my room. He is young and he is smiling. How dare he smile around me! All I want to be is grumpy. He checks my chart and then comes over beside me and says," Well it appears you are starting to whip the infection with a little help from our drugs. You had a pretty nasty infection in that wound. I think that fells who stabbed you put something very infections on the knife blade. I imagine you can be released in a couple of days." With this he turns and walks out of the room.

I start to say something to Chuck only to realize he is no longer here. He must have left while the doctor was blocking my view.

An orderly comes into my room with my breakfast. He sets it up on one of those fool trays that slide over your bed. Then he raises my bed so I am almost in a sitting position. For the first time I realize I'm hungry. In fact, I am famished. No wonder I am in such a grumpy mood. I'm always grumpy when I'm hungry. I wonder how long it has been since I ate. I have no idea how long I was unconscious but from the progress that Chuck told me Mary and Jack have made it must have been for quite some time.

After an untold number of naps, procedures that steal your dignity, smelling of disinfectants, noises that caused me to move to the hill to escape, sleeping in a bed that makes my sleeping bag feel like a foam mattress, and two more days, I am finally released. I know this is a hospital but to me it felt more like a jail.

I find several problems with being released even though I very badly wanted it. I have no transportation. My car is still up at the cabin. I am so weak that the short walk from the bed to the wheelchair, which the hospital insists I must ride in, wears me out. Chuck is waiting to pick me up. He insists that I stay with him and his wife. I have never even met his wife. In the end, I convince Chuck to drop me off at the local motel for tonight. I will worry about tomorrow when it comes.

After I register and get to my room it doesn't take me long to get myself in bed. I don't remember having a single thought after I was in that bed. I must have almost instantly fallen asleep.

I wake up to someone knocking on my door. I guess I should say pounding on my door. I pull on my pants and go to the door. When I open it I find Jack and Mary standing outside. After apologizing for my lack of proper attire, I invite them in. Jack and Mary have looks on their faces like a couple of kids who have just pulled off a successful cookie jar heist. Jack is the first to speak.

"John, we did it. We found Carlo's hidden notebooks. Man what an unbelievable story."

After saying this, he pauses for a long time. I am not a patient man under normal circumstances and these are not normal circumstances so I blurt out, "Come on, Jack, and tell me what this is all about. I would like to know what I have been fighting and just how much more I am going to need to fight. Okay?"

"Okay John, keep your shirt on a minute," then he realizes that I am not wearing a shirt and chuckles a bit. To make matters worse Mary chuckles too. Then, Jack continues with his story.

"Carlo was born in Venezuela. His parents and four brothers still live there, or did. When he was eighteen he got a job on a ship. After he worked on it for a while he ended up in United States. He became an American citizen by joining the army. He learned to fly while he was in the army. He also was taking college courses while he was still in the army. That is where he met his wife. She didn't like the military life very well so he left the service and started his own business of flying precious cargo. Jewelry and documents mostly. His father-in-law financed the operation and was a partner until his health failed."

"I already know most all of this, Jack. Tell me what else you found."

"Okay, here comes the part you don't know. Carlo bought out his father-in-law and ran the business himself. Shortly after this, he was approached by drug smugglers in an effort to get him to fly drugs for them. He refused. A few weeks later the same two guys came back and showed him photos of his brothers in captivity. He thought they were in Columbia. They told him his brothers would be well treated as long as he flew their drugs, but any problem and they would be killed. Carlo was the brains of how to accomplish the smuggling. He increased the size of the engine in his plane and added auxiliary fuel tanks. This way he could file a flight plan and meet its schedule yet fly out of the country to pick up drugs."

"How was he able to get through the radar screen I ask?"

"It wasn't that hard. There are gaps in the radar screen. Now to get back to what I was telling you. Due to the financial strain of starting the business and then later buying out his father-in-law, Carlo's wife had kept her job and home in Saratoga Springs. Carlo found out that the smugglers were not aware of his wife and daughter so he made every effort to keep them from finding out. He was smart enough to know that this arrangement would only last as long as it was beneficial to the cartel. According to his notes, he considered himself, and most likely his brothers, as dead men. He only wanted to protect his wife and daughter. He kept his eyes and ears open and recorded everything he found out in his note book. As time went on the cartel became more trusting and open with him so he was able to gain a great deal of information. Near the end they trusted him enough to have him deliver bribe money to certain recipients. This is how he was able to get the names of politicians, judges, law enforcement personnel and others who were and are involved. Carlo gave his daughter the numbers of his coded message and his wife the clues so if anything happened to him they would have the information needed to bust up this operation. By doing it this way they knew nothing of what was going on and would not be considered accessories in the crimes of the operation. His wife was instructed to take the information to the Drug Enforcement Agency (DEA) if anything happened to him. Evidently the cartel found out about his wife and daughter and started watching them before his wife got the information to the DEA."

"The cartel wanted him to expand his operation so they could deliver more drugs. Carlo refused so they had him killed. His last note said he suspected they had set up an operation based on his methods with another pilot. John, you wouldn't believe what else was in that locker. Cash! Every dollar the cartel had ever paid him was in there."

"What did you do with all of this stuff Jack?"

"We called the FBI and turned it all over to them. They are sorting it all out right now. I think they felt a little sheepish about not believing the information Chuck had given them earlier. However, since Carlo had kept his business financially isolated from the drug business there was no money trail for them to follow. Anyway; I think you and Ginger can breathe easy now."

"So Chuck was right. We were up against a formidable organization. I guess we were lucky to get out of this alive. How did you and Mary ever figure this all out anyway?"

"Mary and I studied the information you gave me and we tried to do what you suggested. We tried to think of how all of this could be fit together to lead us to Carlo's notes. Mary is good at figuring things out. She broke the message down into parts. We finally concluded that Greyhound was most likely the first clue and it would fit the clue "the first is to be expected" so she concluded that this was most likely a route to the location. The second was terminal. We decided that this was most likely the location itself. This needed to fit the clue "the second is simple". After much discussion we decided it must be a station or a depot of some kind. The last was one-one-three this needed to fit the clue "the third repeats itself."

"But this is not the order of the message. One-one-three was the first wasn't it?"

"Yes, we tried to work on it in the order of the message, but got no where so we decided to do it in the order in which we would need to follow to get to the hiding place. You know route, general location and finally, the specific location. Mary got on line and started to plot out the location of every station and depot in Memphis. Then she plotted out every type of storage facility and bank with vault spaces available in Memphis. After she had this accomplished we started trying to find a pattern of one-one-three that repeated itself. At this point we ran into a snag. We could not find this repeat between the stations, depots and storage facilities. We found that most major highways are Greyhound routes so this didn't eliminate many of the locations we had plotted. We concluded that either we were on the wrong track or we were missing something. I suggested we fly to Memphis, rent a car and see what we could find by driving to these locations. We had found three Home Depot store locations which had storage facilities in their same zip code. We decided to start with this. We selected one and went to the storage facility. We found no locker there that matched up with the key we had so we moved on to the second one. There I found a locker that Carlo's key fit and I opened it. The locker number was 226."

"How did you gain access to these places?"

"We just waited until someone punched in the code to open the gate and then we followed them in. To get out we did the same."

"You mean no one challenged you when you were wandering around in there trying your key in every lock?"

"Oh, we were challenged all right. The night manager came up and asked me why I as trying my key in every lock. I told him we had forgotten our locker number. I think he would have called the cops on us, but we got lucky. The key fit the lock I was trying when he walked up. Luckily, he left before I opened the door."

Mary had said nothing during the entire time since they came into my room. Finally, she broke her silence by saying, "I think we had better leave now. John looks rather done in, to say the least."

Jack nodded in agreement and they started toward the door. Just as they reached the door Jack turned and said, "John, I wanted to tell you that Mary and I have become very close. I hope you don't mind. She told me about the night in the cave and how you had held her and comforted her."

"Mind, I not only don't mind I am delighted for both of you. I have always considered myself a married man even though my wife divorced me. She is and always has been my only love. I pray that you two find happiness be it together or apart. Now get out of here. Mary is right. I am beat and need to get some sleep. However; before you leave I would like to ask a favor of you. Will you take me to my cabin tomorrow?"

"Sure, we will pick you up for breakfast about eight-thirty in the morning. Do you think you can be ready by then?"

"Sure, I'll be ready."

Chapter 26

I Get Arrested

I wake up and check the clock. It is a quarter-to-eight. With a great deal of effort I get up and get dressed. There isn't a great deal more I can do to get myself ready for the day. I have only a tooth brush, razor and a comb that I was given by some service organization while I was in the hospital. I don't dare take a shower because of the bandage on my wound so I just wash my face and hands, brush my teeth, shave and pull on my clothes. By now it is nearly eight-thirty. I walk outside to wait for Jack. Jack shows up at eight thirty, sharp. Mary is with him.

I open the back door and get in Jack's rental car. We exchange greetings and nothing else is said. Even after we are in the restaurant no one says anything. Finally the silence gets so thick that it is almost deafening. I break the silence by saying, "Okay Jack, out with it. The look on your face is enough to tell me there is bad news so just go ahead and let me have it."

"Oh, the news isn't all that bad; I talked to Chuck last night about access to your cabin. He told me the only way to get there is still by snowmobile. You know full well you can't ride on one in the shape you are in so I think I will have to go it alone. If you will just give me a list of things you need I will get them for you. Chuck said he had Chigger go up there yesterday to plug the holes in your windows and to change the tank for your heater."

"I got to thinking, last night after you and Mary left. I concluded just what you said about me going up there so I was going to ask you if you would mind going it alone. I think all I need is my computer and its carrying case. I've been in need of some new clothes so I will just buy myself the things I need. I do need some wheels though. Would you take me to the car rental agency before you go up to the cabin?"

Nothing more is said for some time. The waitress comes and takes our order. As she turns to leave I hear a familiar voice saying" Oh, there you are. The Sheriff said I would likely find you here. I have an envelope to give you.

The voice is that of Larry Warner. He hangs around Chuck's office a lot. He serves papers for the court so I pretty well know what is in the envelope. As Larry is handing me the envelope I ask, "What's in the envelope Larry? Is it a subpoena?"

"Well, we will just say it is an invitation with a couple of conditions added to it."

With this Larry turns and walks away. I open the envelope and find that I am to appear in court the day after tomorrow. It also states that I am not to see Ginger until after the court appearance. After I have read it I hand it to Mary. Mary reads it and her face turns bright red. She says nothing. I get the feeling that she is just too much of a lady to say what she is feeling right now.

After we finish our breakfast, Jack takes me to the car rental agency and drops me off. I spend most of the rest of the day renting the car and checking the newspaper for rental houses. By the time I have accomplished these things I am pretty well spent, physically. I return to the motel and take a nice long nap.

After sleeping for about an hour, a knock on the door wakes me up. It is Chuck. He has a look on his face like he would much rather be anywhere else than here. "What's the matter Chuck? You look like you just ate a lemon. Is something wrong?"

"You bet there is Ja. I'm here to place you under arrest. That witch, Ms. Blanchard, insists that you be held on kidnapping charges. The D.A. says that I have to do it since an Amber alert was issued. I guess you had better come along with me."

"Can I grab my toothbrush, razor, and comb first?"

"Sure, grab whatever you want."

I grab my few possessions and head for the door. I had better check out and make arrangements for my car. Is it all right if I do that Chuck?"

"I'll take care of that for you. Just come on before anyone becomes aware of what is going on. We don't need a crowd."

I step through the door and am astonished to find every parking place in the motel lot full. "What's going on here Chuck? Is there some kind of a convention I haven't heard about?"

"No, there is no convention. The word got out that the girl the Amber alert was issued for has been found and the press from almost everywhere came in to report on it. That's why I want to get you to jail before anyone figures out you are the one being held for kidnapping her. This whole mess is getting out of hand and I don't think I can keep a lid on things much longer."

With that, Chuck ushers me to his own personal car. Before I can make a comment Chuck says, "I thought using my own car and not being in uniform might keep people from realizing what I am doing here."

With this we both get in the car and Chuck drives off. When we get to the sheriff's office there are several people standing around near the front door. Chuck just drives on by and turns left at the next corner. He turns up the alley that runs behind his office and parks in the rear. We get out and walk into the office without either of us saying a word. I just walk over to the open cell door and go inside. After standing in the open cell for a few minutes I ask, "Aren't you going to lock the cell door Chuck?"

"No, I'm not. The District attorney may have said I had to put you in jail, but he didn't say anything about me having to lock the door."

Chuck is steamed. I can't recall seeing him this mad unless it was the time when one of his deputies let the mayor's kid go without giving him a speeding ticket, just because he was the mayor's son. I think it is partly because he was told to arrest his friend and partly because things are taking place that he feels are his business to handle yet he has no control over them. Not that Chuck is a control freak. He just likes to feel he is taking care of enforcing the law and that he is not just responding to a bunch of elected officials.

Chuck comes into the cell with me carrying a deck of cards and we play gin rummy until past my bedtime. Chuck finally notices my yawns. He picks up the cards and walks out of the cell.

"I'll be going home now Ja. If anybody bothers you just give me a call. My deputy will be in after he finishes making his rounds. He will see to anything you need. Goodnight."

With that he is out the door and I am sitting alone in an unlocked cell. Oh well, it doesn't matter much to me. I don't plan on going anywhere.

I must have fallen asleep almost as soon as I laid my head down. Anyway I wake up feeling well rested and refreshed. I think I got the best night's sleep I've had in over a week. The bed in this cell is more comfortable that the bed in the hospital and the one in the motel too. The next time I feel the need for a good night's rest I think I will just have Chuck arrest me again.

If Chuck's deputy came in last night I never was aware of it. Anyway Buck comes in carrying my breakfast and a whole pot of coffee.

"Here you go Ja. Chuck said I was to see you got a good breakfast and plenty of coffee. He said to tell you he will be in a little later. He has some things he needs to get straight first."

Knowing Chuck, he is most likely talking to those elected officials and getting control of things back in his own hands or at least making a Herculean effort to do so. I just lean back and enjoy my breakfast and several cups of coffee.

Chuck finally makes it in about two in the afternoon. When he comes through the door he yells for me to meet him in the outer office. When I come through the door to the outer office area Chuck says, "Have a seat Ja." Then he continues, "I managed to get your preliminary hearing set up to take place immediately after the custody hearing. Maybe by this time tomorrow you will be out of jail and back to living your own life. Oh, by the way. I met Jack and Mary at the cafe a while ago. They spent the morning trying to find you. They thought you had fallen off the face of the earth. I explained what had happened and apologized for not letting them know. It just completely slipped my mind. Anyway, they will be stopping by pretty soon. They have news for you about Ginger."

With this said Chuck grabs his hat off of the desk, crams it on his head and goes out the door without even giving me time to respond. Buck, who has been sitting at his desk doing paperwork just shakes his head and says nothing. I wander back to my cell and sit down on the bed.

I am lonesome. For the first time it occurs to me just how much I miss the Kid. I must admit she has gotten under my skin. I can't even imagine how she is feeling right now. I am not sure when her father died, but in the last few months she has lost both her father and her mother. She has been rejected by her grandparents. She has been chased by people trying to kill her. She has found herself dependent on an old man and his friends to help her stay alive. Now she has even been isolated from them. If I know the Kid, she is not taking this too well.

I sit pondering my own thoughts for a while. I have no idea how long, but I heard Chigger relieve Buck. Just a few minutes later I hear someone come in the door. Chigger yells, "Hey Ja, you've got company. Why don't you just come up here and meet them. That cell is no place for entertaining decent folk."

From the voices it is evident that Jack and Mary are here to see me. Maybe now I will find out how the Kid is doing. I get up and walk out into the outer office. Mary looks like she is mad enough to bite nails into pieces. "What's the matter Mary? You don't look too happy, to say the least."

"That's an understatement. I can't figure out what has happened to Ms. Blanchard. I have worked with her for two years now and have always considered her to be reasonable person, but she sure is way off base now. She sees all of us as being a bad influence on Ginger. She won't even agree for me to see her."

"Where is Ginger now Mary?"

"She is with the Marlow family. They are a good family and will treat Ginger very well. I called Liz, that's Mrs. Marlow. She said, "Ginger is being a real handful". She is afraid Ginger will take off if she takes her eye off her for even a few minutes. I told her to treat Ginger like an adult and she may get better results. She said she will try anything because up to now nothing has worked to get Ginger settled in."

"Well, I guess there isn't too much we can do to help Ginger until after the hearing tomorrow. I would like to ask a favor of you two if I may."

"Sure John," Jack responds. "What can we do for you?"

"Go find me a house to rent or, if you can't find a house, find an apartment. I want to be able to say I have a place for Ginger to live beside that cabin up on the mountain. Maybe that will help convince the judge that I am living up to the promises I made. Also, check with the school and see about the testing they were to do. I need to know the status of that before the hearing."

"We can do that John. Do you need anything else?"

"Yeah, there is something. The house or apartment will need to be furnished, but if you can't find one that is furnished then buy the furniture it needs and Mary, I need you to buy Ginger another wardrobe. Get everything she needs. We won't be able to get back to the cabin for some time so she will need several outfits as well as, undergarments, shoes, socks and anything else a girl needs."

"You sure don't ask much do you? It is two-forty-five and most everything closes up at five o'clock in this town as you well know."

"Do what you can. I don't know if I can take it if they take the Kid away from me. For the first time since I came back from Nam I have aspirations. I want to live. I want to raise Ginger. I want to do all kinds of things that I thought I had given up long ago. So please, do the best you can for me and for Ginger too."

Jack is just standing there shaking his head. Mary looks a little overwhelmed too, but at least she is moving toward the door. She looks over her shoulder and says, "Come on Jack, we have a lot to do and not much time to get it done."

While she is saying this she grabs Jack by the sleeve of his jacket and starts dragging him toward the door. In a couple of seconds they are gone so I amble back to my cell. The thing is starting to feel like home. I sure hope I can get over this feeling.

I lie down on the bunk and fall asleep. I wake up a couple of hours later. A short time after I wake up, I hear Chigger leave. I guess he is going out to do his early evening check. Chuck insists that every store be checked to make sure no door is left unlocked. He has this done right after closing time and then a couple of more times during the night.

Chuck comes in and back to my cell. He is carrying a deck of cards.

"Go home, Chuck. You don't need to entertain me."

"I'm not entertaining you. You are to entertain me. My wife has a card group that meets once a week and tonight is the night. I usually come up here just to get away from all the chatter. I saw Chigger making his rounds. I asked him to drop by Mommy's Café and bring us a couple of country fried steaks. He should be here before too long. I hope you are hungry."

We sit playing cards and eating until well past my bed time. Finally, Chuck says, "I guess I can go home now. Surely those ladies have left by this time."

Chapter 27

I Go to Court

I must have fallen to sleep almost as soon as my head hit the pillow. Anyway I don't remember anything after Chuck left until I woke up a few minutes ago. I suppose I had better clean up and get ready. This is the big day. By the time this day is over I will either be a free man, maybe with a child, or I may be preparing to defend myself against some pretty serious charges. I shower and then dress myself in the same clothes I have been wearing for I don't know how many days now. Thanks to Chuck's doing some shopping for me I do have clean socks and underwear. I have almost finished shaving when I hear Chuck come in the front door. I turn as he walks up behind me. He is holding a bright orange jumpsuit.

"I'm sorry Ja, but you will have to wear this to the hearing. I hate to do this but you are being held on some pretty serious charges. It's the rules and I can't do anything about it."

Seeing Chuck's frustration in having to make his friend follow the rules set up for dangerous criminals I say, "Its okay Chuck. I don't want you to break any rules for my sake."

"I know. It is just that this is all so unfair. You should be awarded a metal and instead you are being treated like a criminal. And while we are on the subject of being a criminal I took the liberty of telling your lawyer to show up this morning."

"Robert! He's no criminal lawyer. All he has ever done for me is check over the legal language in some of my contracts. Do you really think I need a lawyer?

"Not for the custody hearing, but I think you should have one at your preliminary hearing on the kidnapping charge. I know that Robert is not a criminal lawyer but he knows his way around in a courtroom and if he thinks you need a criminal lawyer he'll get you one."

"Okay Chuck. You know a lot more about all of this than I do and, by the way, thanks for all you are doing."

About this time Buck comes in with my breakfast. He sets it up in my cell. After putting on the orange jumpsuit I go back to my cell and enjoy breakfast. Chuck joins me in a cup of coffee. He finally stands and says, "Its time to go."

I see the look of distress on his face so I stand and hold my hands out for the cuffs. I figure there is no use making him say the words. Chuck snaps the cuff on me and we head to the back door. Going out the back way doesn't avoid the reporters. They have the back covered as well as the front. Chuck has his deputy go out first to clear us a way to the car. We have no more than stepped through the door than we are bombarded with a barrage of questions.. I make no attempt to answer any of them. The questions are coming so fast that no one would be able to figure out which question I was answering anyway.

Chuck joins me in the back seat of the car. Buck gets behind the wheel and takes us the several blocks to the courthouse. Here, too, reporters are everywhere. Buck gets us through them without too much of a problem.

Chuck leads the way to a small conference room and motions for me to be seated. A few minutes later the judge enters and I rise. He motions for me to be seated. Then Ms. Blanchard comes in and takes a seat. A lady, I think she must be some kind of a court official, comes in and says something to the judge that I cannot hear. The judge gets a look of surprise on his face and says, loud enough that I can plainly hear. "Move to a bigger room! Why this is just a custody hearing. No one will be here for this."

"I'm afraid that the corridor is packed with people insisting to get in Sir," she responds this time loud enough that everyone can hear.

"Well, just tell the reporters they need to select a couple of their number to represent them in the hearing" is the judge's response.

"I'll do that Sir, but there are still way too many people insisting on being seated to fit in this room. I think we will need to move this hearing to a regular courtroom to accommodate all those insisting on being admitted."

"Very well then, move us to a courtroom. We need to get this hearing underway."

With this pronouncement, the judge rises to his feet and leaves the room. The lady who had been talking to the judge directs us to follow her and we move into a courtroom. She seats us in a manner similar to a trial arrangement. Ms. Blanchard sits at the prosecution table. I sit at the defense table and the judge is at the bench.

After looking about the courtroom for a few minutes the judge says, "Okay Ms. Blanchard, you were the one requesting this hearing. Let us hear what you have to say."

Ms. Blanchard slowly rises to her feet, but says nothing for some time. She looks intimidated by the number of people interested in this simple custody hearing. Finally, after an awkward period of silence she finds her voice. "I asked for this hearing because I feel Mr. Davidson is not a fit person to hold custody of a female minor. He is an admitted alcoholic, he is a recluse living in a cabin away from any school or other facility for youth activities, he has spent most of his adult life as a street person, he admits to having abandoned his own family, he has no regular employment and he took the female subject out of our area of jurisdiction without permission. This constitutes kidnapping, Your Honor He is old and from my own experience at the hands of an older man, when I was the age of the child in question, I can only imagine what might be going on when he is with her. Therefore; Your Honor, I request that his custody of the child be withdrawn."

Well, now maybe I understand her feeling about me. Evidently she was molested by an old man when she was a child. The courtroom remains silent, except for an occasional clearing of someone's throat, after Ms. Blanchard finishes talking. After a short period of silence the judge looks over to me and says, "Mr. Davidson would you like to make a response to the statements made by Ms. Blanchard."

"Yes, Your Honor. Everything Ms. Blanchard said is true. I am an alcoholic, sober now for seven years. It is true that I have lived a rather reclusive life during the past five of these years. I did spend most of my adult life living on the streets. It is true that my drinking and inability to deal with post traumatic stress syndrome caused me to abandon my family. I do not excuse myself because of my experiences in Vietnam. Thousands of men shared the same experiences as I, yet they came back and lived normal lives. I did take Ginger out of the area in which I was instructed to remain. I did so because I deemed her life to be in danger and I needed to remove her from harms way. It is true that I am not in the regular employment of anyone or any company. I make my living as an author. This endeavor rewards me with financial benefits well above the average income for this area. I am a Christian and believe in the scriptures. I am familiar with the scripture that says 'it is better to have a millstone tied about your neck and be thrown into the sea than to mislead a child'. Now, if all of this makes me unfit to be the foster parent and, hopefully, someday the parent of Ginger, so be it. But, if caring counts, then I should be permitted to retain custody of Ginger because I truly care. I care enough to give my life to protect Ginger if need be. I also would like to say that for the first time in many years I find I have aspirations. I have aspirations to be a good father for Ginger."

I hold my breath as I sit back down. There is some mumbling in the courtroom. The problem with the seating arrangement is I am unable to see anyone behind me and most everybody is behind me. At least I think there are a number of people back there. The judge breaks the silence by saying, "if there be anyone here who feels they can add to the testimony given you may speak now."

The silence is broken by a number of voices speaking at one time. The judge bangs his gavel on the bench and says, "Silence in the courtroom."

The room again becomes silent except for an occasional cough, or someone shuffling there feet. After a few seconds the Judge says, "Okay Sheriff Hadley you may speak."

"Your Honor I have known John Davidson for the past five years. I make it my business to checkout anyone that moves into my jurisdiction. When John came here I kept an eye on him for a time. He was living in a tent and building his cabin up on the side of Gore Mountain. He was still in withdrawal from alcohol. At times his hands shook so bad he could hardly work on his cabin. I started dropping by and talking to him. He began asking me questions about law enforcement. He used the information I gave him to insure accuracy in the fictional stories he writes. We became friends. When he showed up in my office with Ginger holding his hand and the criminal who had attempted to kill Ginger in the trunk of his car, I felt I could believe what he told me, but I checked it out just the same. All other law enforcement agencies felt it was nothing but a local problem. I felt otherwise and continued the investigation. With the help of John, Mary Lipski and John's friend Jack Anderson we found an extensive drug cartel was trying to kill Ginger as they had killed both her mother and father. If it had not been for the actions of John Davidson, Ginger would have been dead for a couple of weeks by now."

When Chuck was finished the judge pointed to someone else. When they spoke I recognized Mary's voice. She said, "Your Honor. As you know I am the social worker that approved John's application for custody of Ginger. I even found myself in harms way with them for a little over a day. During that day I learned a great deal about Mr. Davidson that you don't learn from the forms prospective foster parents are required to fill out. I was privileged to hear one of the finest father-daughter talks I have ever heard. I found Mr. Davidson to be a gentle man, a man of principle. I found him to be extremely protective of Ginger. Mr. Davidson has rented a house here in town and has made arrangements for Ginger's schooling. I not only would recommend that he remain the foster parent of Ginger, but that he be allowed to adopt her. Thank you for your attention Your Honor."

Again the judge pointed his finger at someone and said, "you Ms. did you have something you wanted to say."

"Yes, Your Honor. I am the daughter of John Davidson. I just wanted to say that from all I know about him he was a good father and husband until he could no longer bear the burden of Vietnam. My mother gave us a number of papers he wrote during his college years and the years he taught. They were a great deal of help in molding our lives. Though I hardly know him in person I respect him for his values. I think it was the conflict of these values and the reality of war that nearly destroyed him. I respect him for how he has managed to put his life back together and I am looking forward to getting to know him in person. The person I have known only by the words of my mother and the words he wrote so long ago."

I can hardly believe my ears. My daughter is here and she doesn't hate me for abandoning her, her sister and their mother. She actually wants to get to know me. This is even more than I had dared to dream for.

About this time Robert Milton, my lawyer comes in and sits down beside me. Then the judge again points to someone and says, you; the lady in the blue suit. Do you have something to add?"

"Yes, your honor. I am the wife John abandoned. I just wanted to say John is a good man. I watched him wake up screaming the name of his friends. Most were friends who died in Vietnam. I listened as he tossed about in his sleep talking of unspeakable things that happened. He would have been appalled had he known that I heard all of these events. I marvel at how he has brought his life back together. I only fault him in as much as he didn't have the faith in me to let me help him. I want you and all concerned to know that if John needs or desires help raising Ginger, I will be honored if he calls upon me for that help."

Again there is silence in the courtroom. The judge scans the courtroom for a few moments then he says, I know that many of you have not been given an opportunity to speak, but I have heard enough." He pauses for a couple of seconds then he says, "I shall render my ruling."

"From the testimony delivered here today I have concluded that John Davidson is a good man who has overcome great problems. Problems most of us have not been asked to face. Further, he is dedicated to the protection of the female child in his custody, dedicated to the point that he has risked his life more than once to protect her. If he had not done so she would likely not be alive today. I have been given assurance that he can support his ward well and has the intention to do so. I find that John Davidson should retain custody of Ginger Rodriguez. Now I believe we have a preliminary hearing regarding charges of kidnapping brought against John Davidson. Mr. District Attorney are you prepared?"

"Yes, Your Honor we are. The office of the District Attorney, after making an extensive investigation, finds the charges brought against John Davidson are not warranted and we wish to withdraw all charges"

The judge, with a smile on his face, says, "Then Mr. Davidson I suggest that after the sheriff is finished with your processing you pick up your foster daughter and go on with your life."

I want to talk to my wife and daughter, but when I turn I find the court room to be so packed that I will be unable to get through the crowd of people and furthermore I can't see them or maybe it is that I can't recognize them. Instead I turn to Robert and say. "Thanks for coming Bob. I am glad your services weren't need today. Send me a bill and I will drop by and pay you."

"There will be no bill for this John. I felt privileged to sit with you here. We will just chalk this up to a friend helping a friend."

Chuck looks over to Buck and says, "Buck you get this crowd out of here so we can get Ja over to pick up Ginger. I don't care what you have to do to get them out of here I just want them gone now."

Buck says nothing. He just walks outside and is gone for no more than five minutes. When he returns he says, "Chuck, I would wait about five more minutes for the traffic to clear out of here then I think we will be able to go without much bother."

CHAPTER 28

WITH ASPIRATIONS FOUND

After waiting about five minutes Buck starts toward the door. The corridor is clear except for some photographers. When we get outside, there is no crowd and cars are scurrying in every direction.

Chuck looks astonished and says, "What the heck did you do Buck? I hope you didn't spread the rumor that we have smallpox here or something."

"Nah, boss, I just took the bullhorn outside and told them there would be a press conference in an hour in front of the Sheriff's office and until that time anybody trying to ask questions would be ignored. I thought that would give us enough time to go pick up Ginger."

Buck sometimes talks like a total dodo but he is a smart man. I sometimes think he puts on the dumb act just to get people to underestimate him.

Chuck and I get into the back seat and Buck drives off toward the Marlow's house. It is about a ten minute ride to get there, but time always passes slowly when you are in a hurry.

When Buck pulls up in front of the Marlow's, Mrs. Marlow and Ginger are standing on the porch waiting for us. I guess Mary must have called her.

I step out of the car door and Ginger comes running towards me. When she is about half way across the yard she stops, turns, hesitates and then runs back and gives Mrs. Marlow a hug. I thought to myself the Marlows must be very special people it they could win Gingers affection while she was being forced to be where she didn't want to be. After giving Mrs. Marlow a hug, she runs as fast as she can back to me. When she reaches me she jumps up wrapping her legs around my waist and her arms around my neck. She hugs me so tight it is almost like being in the squeeze of an anaconda. After returning the hug I peel her off of me and put her in the car.

As Buck pulls away and starts toward the sheriff's office Ginger looks over at me and says, "nice suit Old Man, but I don't really think orange is your color.

Chuck smiles and then says, "He won't be wearing it much longer Ginger. As soon as we get back to the office he can change out of these coveralls and get back to being his normal, dapper self."

This brings a smile to Ginger's face. She has never seen me dressed in anything but jeans and a flannel shirt.

Ginger says in a hateful tone of voice, "Why did that old witch stick me in another foster home and have you thrown into jail anyway. Is she some kind of a sicko or something?"

"Don't judge, Ms. Blanchard too harshly Kid. She was just trying to protect you from the kind of horror she was put through by an old man when she was your age."

"Maybe she thought she was doing the right thing but she took me away from you when you were the only one who had been protecting me. Didn't she realize the danger she put me in to say nothing of the danger she put the Marlow's in?"

"She, like most of the law enforcement agencies, didn't believe there was a viable threat to either of us. I am sure she would do nothing intentionally to put you in harm's way."

All too soon, Buck turns the corner by the sheriff's office and then into the alley behind the sheriff's office. Before he turns, I can see a crowd of people standing nearby. I guess these are the ones waiting for the press conference that Buck promised them. I appreciated his getting the crowd dispersed but I sure am not looking forward to facing this mob of reporters.

When Buck parks behind the sheriff's office I am pleasantly surprised to see only a few photographers at the back door. We step out of the car and go in the back door. Chuck looks over at me and says, "Go get into your own clothes. Jack and Mary brought you some new ones. You'll find them in the cell you were kept in. I'll go out and warm up the audience for you."

"Yeah, you do that Chuck. There's nothing I hate more than playing to a cold audience."

It doesn't take me long to change into my own clothes and rejoin Ginger. Chuck is outside talking to the crowd. Ginger and I step through the door and listen to Chuck.

"This morning I had the unpleasant duty of taking my friend to court in a jumpsuit and handcuffs. I am happy to say he was found to be innocent of any wrongdoing and also found to be worthy to continue acting as the foster father of his ward Ginger Rodriguez. The Amber alert, which I assume is what brought you here, was issued when John Davidson took Ginger out of the jurisdiction set by our court, without first seeking permission from the Children and Family Services. It was found that Mr. Davidson did this for Ginger's protection. I know you are aware of some of the circumstances in this case. I am not at liberty, to any great extent, to talk about this case because there are several agencies actively involved in investigating the circumstances and the crimes involved. I am at liberty to tell you Gingers parents were both killed by members of a drug cartel. This cartel has pursued and attempted to capture or kill Ginger for over two weeks now. John Davidson found Ginger nearly frozen and took her in. Since that time he has protected her from the men with intent to do her harm. Through the actions of John Davidson and his friends, we have been able to gather enough information that both state and federal agencies are now involved in this investigation."

Chuck's statement is followed with what seems like an endless barrage of questions. I must admit that Chuck handles the questions well. I never knew he was such an accomplished public speaker. Finally Chuck calls an end to the questions. By this time he is answering most of them with either "I don't know or I am not at liberty to answer that at this time."

All the time Chuck was talking I kept scanning the crowd to see if my ex-wife and daughter might be in the crowd. I am never able to find them. Chuck hands me the microphone. I feel awkward and totally unprepared to talk to this crowd. I have done practically no public speaking since my teaching days. Finally I find the strength to speak and say, "I can add very little to what Sheriff Hadley has told you. However, I would like to ask a favor of you. Ginger missed her mother's funeral because we were running from those wishing to do her harm at the time of the funeral. I promised her that I would take her to her mother's grave site. I would appreciate it if you would provide her with the private time she deserves to tell her mother goodbye."

There are several attempts to ask questions, but I ignored them until someone asked if Ginger would say something. To this I responded, "It is up to Ginger."

Ginger reaches over and takes the microphone in her small hand and says. "It has been a long and arduous ordeal. I just want to say that I appreciate all of those who have helped me. I would appreciate the private time that my father requested for me. I just want you to know that I am all right and I will be all right, because for the first time in my life I know that I am and that I have been loved. Thank you."

With this she lays the microphone on the podium, turns and walks through the door back into the sheriff's office. I turn and follow her.

Chuck says, "Chigger brought you your rental car. It is parked in the back of the office. Here are your keys."

Ginger and I walk through the office and out toward the car. Jack and Mary are standing beside it. Jack looks up and says," Well John, I think I will be flying out of here soon. I don't know how long the magazine will wait for me to make the photo shoot they have already paid me to do, but I think I had better go earn my money. Do you need anything before I leave?"

"No Jack, I think you have done quite enough. Besides, if I am reading the look in your and Mary's eyes correctly I expect I will be seeing a great deal of you for a while."

Jack opens his mouth as if to say something, but Mary speaks first. "You bet you will. Now be off and on your way. You have a promise to keep."

"Thanks Mary for everything and as for you Jack, I promise that if we ever get in a gun battle together again I won't take time out for a nap in the middle of the fight. Okay?"

"Okay buddy. I will hold you to that and good hunting."

"Good hunting to you, Jack"

With this Ginger and I get into the car and drive away. By the time we reach the highway we have a procession behind us longer than a military convoy on the way to summer camp. Neither Ginger nor I say anything. I guess we are each lost in our own thoughts. I am wondering how I will ever be able to find my family again. I feel badly that I did not have an opportunity to talk to them and thank them for standing up for me. I can hardly believe they don't hate me after my leaving them and never returning. I feel like the world's luckiest man. I guess that if Jack, Mary and I were able to find Carlo's hiding place then I should be able to find my family.

I turn off the main highway and down the street to the cemetery. When we get to the turn for the cemetery entrance there are local police cars parked on the grass either side of the gate. A policeman motions us through but stops all of the traffic behind us. I am sure that Chuck set this up. I owe that man a lot. I continue to drive until I reach the plot Mary had mapped out for me. I park the car and get out. The snow is not nearly as deep here as it was on the mountain. I walk around and open the door for Ginger. She steps out and puts her small soft hand into my much larger and rather callused hand. We walk, hand in hand, until we are at the foot of her parent's graves. Ginger stands silently for some time then she looks up at me and asks, "Do you think my parents are in heaven?'

"I have no way of knowing that Ginger. I do know that God loves those who love and he has a special place in his heart for those who love enough to give their own life to protect the life of another. So I would guess that he will meet you parents with open arms."

"My parents did love me, didn't they John?"

"Yes Ginger, your parents loved you so much that they were willing to die for you. Circumstances and some bad people put your parents in a very strange and dangerous position. Because of these circumstances they were not in a position to show you just how much they loved you."

"I think you should say a prayer over my parent's graves. Would you do that for me?"

"I agree that a prayer should be said over your parent's graves, but I think you should say it."

"I don't know how to pray. I wouldn't know what to say."

"Just say whatever you would like to say to God. Talk to him just like you would talk to me except maybe with a little more respect."

I have hardly finished saying this when Ginger kneels down tugging on my hand indicating I should kneel to show respect also. I fall to my knees and fold my hands just as she has. Then Ginger begins to pray saying, "God, I want you to take my parents to live with you. They may not have known you, but they were very good people and I think heaven will be a better place if they are there. Thank you, God, for letting me have such good parents and for letting me have my new father. Amen"

When Ginger finished praying we remained kneeling for some time. Finally, she stands and I stand with her. We start walking back toward the car and I become aware that someone or maybe even more that one is following us. About the time I am turning to look my wife or ex-wife catches up to us. She walks up beside Ginger and takes her by the hand.

"Would you like some help raising Ginger, John?"

"Sure I would Karen, but what will your husband think about this?"

"Edward died three years ago. Besides I never misled him to believe I had ever stopped loving you. He knew that I still loved you and married him only because I could no longer have you."

I continued to have this feeling that someone is behind me. I glanced over my shoulder and find that my daughters are both behind us. I look over at Karen and ask, "Do we have grandchildren?"

"Yes, we have five grandchildren. Three girls and two boys, but if you want to spoil grandchildren with neat children's toys you will need to wait for Ginger to give us more grandchildren. The ones you have are all teenagers."

I look down at Ginger and ask, "Do you and your sisters mind if I kiss my wife." All three nodded in the affirmative.

THE END

978-0-595-71981-5
0-595-71981-3

Printed in the United States
112612LV00005B/13/P

9 780595 719815